How to Housetrain Your Husband

RACHELLE BARRETT

Rachelle Barrett

HOW TO HOUSETRAIN YOUR HUSBAND

Contents

This book is dedicated to the ladies that inspired its creation in no particular order:

Jennifer Fischer, Lindsay Son, Laurie Sprauer, Kristy Olsen and Katie Blaser.

And to Kevin who was allowed to read it if he only had nice things to say. :)

This book was a product of fiction even though it was inspired by the silly shenanigans of real people. It was a labor of love to write. It was also a terror to bring to print, since I had no idea what I was doing. I appreciated the guidance of the lovely writers groups and readers groups on the internet, Powell's books, and the encouragement of my friends and family to complete a goal I set for myself.

If you like this book, tell me to keep writing. And if you didn't like this book, use it as a paperweight or give it away at a garage sale. My lovely daughter Maya Barrett did the art for the cover and I would hate to see that go to waste.

Chapter 1

Then and Now

Once upon a time Candace, Miriam, Lucy and I sat fully clothed together in the copper soaking tub of a lushly appointed Las Vegas Hotel room discussing whether or not anal sex was an ok line to cross in a loving committed relationship.

Candace: Of course you will like it. Once your pussy gets tired, the fudge factory feels like a virgin again.

Miriam: Do you even remember what it felt like to be a virgin? That was not pleasant.

Lucy: I am gonna need more Pork Rinds if I have to listen to Candace and my brother's sexcapades again.

Me: I just keep hearing Johnny Cash's "Burning Ring of Fire" play in my head every time he goes for the brown.

Lucy: *Crunch*

Miriam: *Sob* Let's be friends forever.

Candace: Ok, time for bed Miriam.

***

Ten years and a couple of kids later, while our friendship was still strong, our vaginas were another matter. Our conversations had changed just a wee bit and get-togethers like Vegas took more than an act of congress to organize.

Me: My least favorite chore is, hands down, cleaning the dishes.

Lucy: The animals and their various hidey holes in my house.

Candace: How many do you have now, Luce?

Lucy: Too many.

Miriam: Laundry. I can't even describe the odor coming off of Bobs' socks after basketball without wanting to throw up in my mouth.

Candace: Driving the kids to their activities five days a week and then standing outside during soccer practice pretending I give a damn that Joey has punched that kid in the throat again.

Miriam: Don't you?

Candace: No. He's finally tall enough to fend for himself. I am proud.

We had at least managed to organize a bi-weekly lunch date at the Cheesecake factory that was 10 minutes from Candace's bookshop She Reads and 15 minutes from the satellite campus where I adjunct taught for the Chemistry department for State University. Both Lucy and Miriam worked from home, which meant they could set their own hours and would be the subjects of merciless ridicule if they missed our lunch date. The lunch that started the experiments began like any other.

Miriam: Why don't we do this more often?

Lucy: Traffic.

Me: Statistically, we should do it more often. The 60 minutes we spend here and in traffic is roughly 4% of the day. Or if we calculate by the week … 0.6% which is barely anything when you consider how much time in a person's life is spent watching television.

Candace: Nerd.

Miriam: 4% of a day spent on something just for me sounds really sad when you put it into perspective.

Lucy: What about the time you spend at the gym? Isn't that you time?

Miriam: Do I look like I go to the gym more often than I see you ladies for lunch?

Candace: Luce, only you would think working out counts as "Me Time".

Lucy: I happen to thrive on the adrenaline rush I get from exercise.

Me: I can think of some other things I would rather do to get an adrenaline rush.

Miriam: You are inhuman if you think running out of breath on a bike that isn't going anywhere is an adrenaline rush.

Lucy threw a French fry at Miriam.

Lucy: What about sleeping? Does that count as "Me Time" for you three?
Miriam: *Sigh* sleeping through chainsaw Bob is not "Me Time" either. God, I miss business trips.

Miriam downed the rest of her non-alcoholic strawberry tea as if it were a shot of tequila.

Candace: Separate sleeping spaces have certainly done wonders for my marriage.
Lucy: How did you manage that, Candy? Jonas needs to cuddle with the lights on for a good fifteen minutes before falling blissfully to sleep.
Me: Maybe you should try the Cry- it- Out method on your husband.

I had no idea that what I had said in an offhand comment would start The Experiments. But then again, I rarely know what is going through someone else's head when they listen to me, as evidenced by the number of students currently failing my Chemistry Level 2 course. While Miriam tried desperately to stifle the juice shooting out of her nose in her laughter, Lucy had latched on to something.

Lucy: How would that go? I didn't even successfully sleep train the twins.

Candace: You have two six -year -old girls and a husband sharing that bed of yours?

Lucy: No, just the husband. The girls moved out to their own place when they turned five. Something about their creativity being stifled.

Miriam: You could always stifle Jonas.

Candace: But then our next lunch would be visiting Lucy in jail.

Me: Does anyone here like sleeping with their husband?

Candace: Well, I do enjoy burying my ice cold toes in that spot behind Paul's knees and listen to him squeal like a stuck pig.

Miriam: Bob says the coldness of my toes defies physical nature.

Me: That might just be Lucy's answer.

Lucy: We could Sleep Train them all.

Miriam: We could House train them.

Me: Like a series of experiments. Report the results to each other, reflect, adjust until we get the appropriate outcomes.

Candace: You're not going to write a research paper on our husbands, are you Jenna?

Me: I could if our results are sound.

Lucy: If I get a good night's sleep, our results are sound.

Miriam: Ditto.

Me: First step, Lucy's icy foot bath.

Miriam: Next step, The World. I have always wanted to say that.

Chapter 2

Sleep Training
Your Husband

The most important thing for any person's sanity is a good night's sleep. Lack of sleep has been linked to heart disease, diabetes, increased violence, car accidents, child abuse, increased illness, obesity and reduced sex drive, or so WebMD says. Too many women share a bed with an uncooperative bed partner. The reduced brain power accompanying insufficient sleep might be the reason for the glass ceiling in the business world. Once the sleep problem is solved, who knows what other limitations we could overcome?

The plan to sleep train a husband was as simple as the scientific method: 1) Define the type of sleeper he is 2) Identify the type of sleeper you need him to be 3) Investigate the gap between the two 4) Hypothesize a solution 5) Try the solution 6) Adjust as necessary.

Introducing Jonas the Overzealous Cuddler. Jonas had a lot to say, and he saved it all for his wife at bedtime. He jabbered into her saintly ear on a myriad of subjects from work at the taxi garage, to acquiring peace in Croatia, to Libyan Literature. He held his bride in his arms, his torso firmly pressed to her backside as his body heat slowly cooked her in her skimpy tank top and shorts. Red faced and breathing heavy, Lucy stared at the wedding pictures pasted perfectly symmetrically on the bedroom wall mumbling noncommittal grunts of affirmation until Jonas' waterfall of words slowed to a trickle. Just as his words stopped and his breathing deepened into an even rhythm, his arms suddenly tightened on her bony hips like a vise made of Adamantium.

Need: shut up and give me some space

Lucy is a hot sleeper and so is Jonas, which would not have made them a match on any dating website, but it is what it is.

Gap: I wish there was one

Hypothesis: freezing feet make a spouse intolerable to cuddle. More space means more sleep.

Execution:....

First, Lucy gave their daughters a healthy dose of sugar right before bedtime. Next, she convinced Jonas that she was testing a new body-soothing footbath for the *Sunbody* Business she bought into. Alone in the bathroom, she acquired the square tub that came home from the hospital with the birth of the twins– "it is not stealing if it is covered by insurance". She filled it with a mixture of ice cubes, water, and lavender salt (for believability). Then from inside of the locked bathroom she shouted at him to put the girls to bed.

To which he replied that bedtime could wait until she was done with whatever she was doing.

To which she replied that he should get off of his phone and "spend some time with your children, you lazy fuck."

To which he replied, "Language." She also heard the satisfying sound of a cellphone being docked in its charging station followed by a herd of elephants stomping up the stairs. The sounds of the children's gleeful shrieks that Daddy was putting them to bed for once provided the perfect muffle for the shrieks Lucy admitted after she built up the courage to actually submerge her overwarm toes in the ice bath.

Lucy knew that for maximum effectiveness she should keep her feet in the water for as long as she could stand it, however the tears pooling in the corners of her eyes quickly told her that two minutes was about as long as she could stand it. She removed her feet from the bath, with a hissed breath of relief, to the pre-placed towel.

She could hear from Jonas' voice in the twins' room that the fiendish twins had not made it actually into their beds yet. She proceeded to do a few squats, then a wall sit, and a countertop push up. When she bent down to stretch her hamstrings, she noticed that her feet were completely warmed up again. Dammit!

She decided to try the stretches with the feet submerged to balance the body heat from the workout with the frigid temperature of the water. Another shriek escaped as the feet went back in. All of a sudden, the bathroom door flew open, bumping her butt and causing her to overbalance with a summersault into the bathtub. "Are you ok? I heard a scream."

Lucy sputtered strands of her own hair out of her mouth. "I was fine. Now I think I might have sprained by butt."

"If I weren't so tired, I would take that as an invitation," he grinned, leveraging her out of the bathtub.

A quick stretch to check the temperature of her feet, then she limped to follow him to the bed. Part of the plan had already worked. Getting the girls to bed would wear out a marathoner much less a lightweight like Jonas. She was already hopeful that the conversation would be cut short tonight.

Under the covers, she faced toward him, planting her frigid feet into the small of his back. He hissed, then retreated to the very edge of his side of the bed. She flipped over to turn out her bed table lamp, feeling victory in her grasp. She was thwarted when he flipped over to face her, lowering his arm vice-like arm down over her torso. Not done in quite yet, she channeled her yoga instructor's voice "Tight little ball" and scrunched her feet upward and behind so that they rested squarely on his delicate ball sack. His grip loosened as his arm swooped downward to protect the seat of his manhood.

Lucy smiled to herself in the dark, then snuggled into her pillow, preparing for sleep. Jonas' slurred voice cracked the blessed silence. "The girls were so cute..."

So she did the only thing she could think to do in the moment. She began a diatribe describing the contents of her favorite nutritional supplements and their current FDA status, in alphabetical order. He was snoring lightly after Ginseng. Happily, Lucy joined him in slumber, hanging a single foot outside of the covers for insurance.

Evaluation: Hypothesis of cold feet creating space was a success. Needed: the adjustment for talking.

Introducing Bob, the **Suffocating Bear**. Bob has always slept like the dead. Once in college, the dorm next door to his caught fire. The residents were moved into the various rooms of Bob's dorm during the night. Bob awoke the next morning with no idea who the person asleep on his floor was. When Miriam's son was born, she was up with him every night for the first 6 months for changes and feedings. Bob, meanwhile, regaled everyone within hearing about what a champion sleeper his newborn son was. I happen to know that the kid had cholic. To give Bob his due, it also impressed him how beautiful his wife had become since birthing his child. Apparently, when a curly haired Mexican woman stops brushing her hair for six months, beautiful ringlets form.

Need: silence please

Sleep training Miriam's son consisted of a two-night spa vacation for Miriam, leaving Bob in charge of the baby. Bob slept through the whole thing. After Miriam came home from the spa, her son and husband slept like champs, but poor Miriam, used to the midnight wake ups, found herself awake at one in the morning next to a suffocating bear. No really, she recorded the sounds Bob makes while snoring and it sounds like a zoo animal. Over the last two years, she had become an avid midnight Telenovela watcher and devoted afternoon napper. Our lunch date really pulled her out of her routine.

Gap: He sleeps, I don't.

Hypothesis: If the snoring stops, sleep will happen.

After playing us the tape, that she had also cleverly remixed over a reading of the Hatchet, Candace suggested Bob seek a sleep specialist. Miriam was pretty sure the kind of insurance they were on would not cover that. We had some additional suggestions she might try before spending that money.

1. Reposition

The first night of the reposition experiment, Miriam waited for Bob to fall to sleep while reading a new Julia Quinn book recommended by Candace. Once the snoring began, she used her arm strength to leverage Bob onto his side, facing away from her. She lined pillows between them from head to Bob's bubble butt. As she stacked the

final pillow into place, Bob rolled onto his back, squash-
ing Miriam and, more importantly, Miriam's arm beneath
him. The vibrations coming from Bob's snores moved up
Miriam's arm, sending it to tingling. No matter how she
tried, she couldn't pull it loose. No sleep for Miriam.

The second night of the reposition experiment, she
added tennis balls to the inside of Bob's pajama shirt.
She quickly removed her arm from range. This time
when he rolled onto his back, his torso was more open,
allowing the snores to fill with the power of his whole
diaphragm and echo off of the walls. The balls did make
it easier to move him for some reason, so she was able to
add enough pillows to firmly move him to his side. Once
propped on his side, the dying Bear sound lessened, but
now there was not enough room on the bed for Miriam.
Exhausted with her efforts, Miriam vacated to her couch
and her Telenovela.

The third night, she got the balls and pillows in place
with less hassle than the previous nights. She was also
prepared with a few of his silk ties to affix him to the
bedpost. Once secured, she was removing the pillows to
make room for herself on the bed when Bob woke up.
Thinking his wife had developed a sudden taste for kink,
they had a wild night that ended with Miriam tied to the
bedpost and Bob snoring.

2. Avoid Deep Sleep

An internet search suggested that Bob's ability to achieve deep sleep was assisting the snoring. So the only logical suggestion was to keep him from achieving deep sleep. We helped Miriam to gather supplies. When she suggested smelling salts made of ammonia house cleaning products, Lucy nixed that idea in favor of some potent essential oils. Candace suggested a feather, ice pack and flash light. Every hour that night Miriam poked, prodded, feathered and shone a light into Bob's eyeballs. She quickly rolled over to feign sleep just before Bob came awake. He didn't snore all night. He didn't sleep either, and neither did Miriam. After she and Bob got into some huge fight about the appropriate time it takes to wilt spinach, Miriam abandoned this approach.

3. Clear the Nostrils

To make up for the deep sleep avoidance fiasco, I bought Miriam a pack of Breathe right strips. When she told him what it was for, he dutifully placed the strip over his bulbous Italian nose. The strip itched, but being the loving, supportive husband that he is, Bob did not complain. Once asleep, he flopped to and fro on his pillow like a fish out of water. The jerky movements ended up with an elbow in Miriam's face and the strip sweated off and stuck to the pillow where it did no one any good. The next morning, Miriam sported a bruise on her forehead resembling a unicorn horn and promptly threw the rest of the pack in the garbage can.

She suggested the next night that he take a hot shower to clear his sinuses instead. Bob, being a firm believer in morning showers, due to the aforementioned sweating, and also the one who paid the water bill, needed some enticement to partake of a steamy night time shower. And while his snoring was considerably less after the shower, Miriam and Bob will be expecting their next bundle of joy in June.

Evaluation: Showers reduce snoring in bear men but may result in pregnancy. Adjustment to hearing needed.

I bought Miriam an early baby shower present of Bluetooth earbuds that play soothing ocean waves. She's getting used to them while Bob cheerfully snores away like a Suffocating Loveable Bear.

Introducing Paul, **The Couch Sleeper**. Paul works the long hours of a surgeon and keeps funny eating habits because of it. Being a parent wasn't supposed to disrupt his life and so far it hadn't. A typical evening found Candace clearing the dishes from the meal she made from scratch that she and the three children enjoyed when Paul arrived home. He checked on their son Joey's progress on his homework, making a correction here and there, read a Medical Journal while Karin splashed in her bath, then fell to sleep watching a chipmunk movie with Harriet on the couch.

Need: to feel like a desirable woman who sleeps with her husband

Candace shooed the older children to their beds, leaving Harriet asleep nestled beneath a blanket at her father's feet. Virtually alone, except for the snoring duo on the couch, she poured herself a glass of wine, picked out a book from the kitchen shelf and left the room with a small light on in the bathroom to serve as a night light along with the flickering screen of the television. She knew that Joey would wake Paul at 6 in the morning when he came down to rummage in the cabinet, packing his lunch for school and fixing his breakfast. At some point in the night, Harriet would wake up uncomfortable and seek her out in her fluffy queen bed. Then Candace would sleep the sticky sleep of child hood cuddles.

Gap: Harriet

Candace didn't think anything was wrong with their sleeping situation. Harriet has been a terrible sleeper since the moment she exited the womb. With two other children to contend with, Candace didn't have the energy to deal with sleep training. Plus a slight enjoyment of the discomfort Paul had eventually succumbed to, Harriet became a co-sleeper with Candace's blessing. We encouraged Candace to try some experimenting to see if Paul's and by extension her sleeping could be improved. Considering that Harriet was a kindergartener this year and asking for sleepovers, Candace reluctantly agreed.

Hypothesis: If they get Harriet out of their bed and Paul into it, better sleep can be had by all.

1. Apply smelling salts

Like Miriam with Bob, Candace needed supplies to get him moved from that couch. The first night the smelling oils worked to wake Paul, but Candace had forgotten to move sleeping Harriet from her balled position under the blanket at her father's feet first. Harriet fell to the ground when Paul jerked awake. Paul, of course, comforted his daughter through another movie on the couch until she fell back to sleep in her father's arms, tears drying on her cherubic cheeks.

2. Remove child then apply smelling salts

The second night, they removed Harriet to a mattress on Karin's floor where she slept amid a pile of half constructed Legos. Smelling salts again were applied to Paul, who woke confused and childless. He allowed Candace to guide him up the stairs to their bed. Comfortably ensconced beside her husband on the bed, Candace picked up the book she meant to review for the amateur author she was featuring in the store later in the week. The light might have been too much for Paul, who eventually left the bed to return to his couch, flipped on the television, and passed out to a MythBusters episode.

3. Remove the child, then apply smelling salts, add wine

The third night, instead of going for her book, after application of smelling salts, Candace poured Paul a glass of wine and one for herself served in the bedroom which they promptly spilled on the white down comforter of their bed. They stripped the bed and tossed the comforter into the washer for cleaning. They both fell to sleep on the couch to the MythBusters episode while waiting for the dryer to finish.

4. Remove the child, then apply smelling salts, add porn

The fourth night Candace cued up a porn in the bedroom before moving Harriet, pouring the wine and waking Paul. He was more than happy with this turn of events until Harriet also woke up from a nightmare needing comfort.

Evaluation: If a married couple attempts to watch porn with children home, said children will ruin the experience, and all others. Also, MythBusters induces sleep in uncomfortable settings.

At this point, Candace told us to stop interfering with the good thing she had going before the experiments. As far as I know, Paul is still sleeping on the couch and Candace gets good sleep with Harriet in the bed.

Introducing Clifford, **The Sleep Sexer**. They didn't believe me after I told them why our children never shared our bed. Frankly, I was embarrassed to tell them, knowing full well the jokes that would follow Clifford around at the next game night, with him none the wiser. My friends have the senses of humor of pubescent school children. Candace demanded that I share because of all that we put her through with nothing to show for it except a clean comforter.

There was a stunned silence around the table after I finished telling them. We sipped our iced teas. I wished mine was of the long island variety, but work wasn't over for the day.

Candace: So every time you turn out the light?

Me: Unless he is sick.

Lucy: And you let it happen?

Me: Well, I can redirect if I am really not in the mood.

Miriam: Is it good?

Me: Not as good as when he's awake. He has much more finesse then. But, I don't know. When he's asleep, he doesn't say anything at all and it's kind of like being with a stranger.

Lucy: So he doesn't remember anything.

Miriam: How can you tell he is not actually awake?

Candace: You know. I saw something like this on 20-20.

Lucy: How is his stamina?

Miriam: Lucy!

Candace: It doesn't sound like you have much of a problem. You still get to fall to sleep afterward.

Me: Yeah, but it subtracts about an hour and a half of good sleep.

Lucy: An hour and a half? Jesus!

Me: Well, there's post-coital clean up, and reducing my heart rate enough that I can shut my brain down. Sometimes I have to get a book back out and read some more to shut my brain down and then when I turn off the light again, Round Two.

Miriam: Omigod

Candace: Ok, I know the answer: sleeping pills.

Lucy: For which one?

Candace: Both.

Me: Not very imaginative.

Need: Cleanliness in order to sleep

Here is what I told them. Clifford and I had a night-time ritual that started when we were both in Grad school. We would lie in bed with our bed side lamps on reading whatever texts we are on to see who could out-last who before being bored to sleep. Only, I always won because I couldn't quite get my brain to shut down until I reached the next official stopping point in the text. When I got there, I shut off the light and then there was a whole breathing/meditation thing to get my brain to stop wondering about work or the meaning of the uni-verse or what I should pick up for dinner the next night. Yoga really helped with this process, I swear. Immedi-ately when the lights turned out, however, my husband, in his sleep, reached a clumsy hand over to my side of the bed and began to fondle me.

He then climbed on top of me and made love to me. Afterward I had to leave the bed, because I didn't want to sleep in the dripping juices of our lovemaking all night, cleaned myself up and started the whole breathing/meditation thing again until morning.

Gap: Clifford's semen

Hypothesis: first one to sleep stays asleep

1. Unsexy Inaccessible pajamas

For my experiment, I opted for Fort Knox pajamas. It was winter after all. Target had a sale on adult onesies in a variety of animals. The moment my light went out after a satisfying chapter on the effect of pH on body kinetics, I knew I had made a miscalculation. There was a large zipper on my onesie that traveled the length of my body from breasts to thighs. Apparently, my insatiable sleeping husband could work a zipper very well in his sleep.

2. Chemical enhancement

Lucy gave me some aroma therapy she assured me would aid in sleep. I wouldn't try sleeping pills because I had high blood pressure already and my medication did not agree with certain sleep aids. She told me to spray a little bit onto my pillow and skip the book. The key to our plan was for me to fall to sleep before Clifford.

To aid in our endeavor, I might have also added some coffee beans to the pepper dry rub I put on his steak that evening. We lay in bed and I shut out my light. I tried not to sneeze from the scent wafting up from my pillow. Why was Chamomile supposed to be conducive to good sleep? I rolled away from Clifford, but that put my head directly into the pillow, which made my eyes water. Perhaps I used too much. I felt myself suffocating, so I shifted positions again just to find myself staring at Clifford as he read. He felt me looking at him, so I squeezed my eyes shut before they caught me. I began to count Supreme Court Justices in order from swear in date.

Mercifully, his light shut off. Then a hand snaked across my belly. Miriam's question came back to me. Was he awake all of those times? His fingers dipped into the waistband of my pants. I thrust away from his probing hand, donkey-kicking him in the process with a satisfying oof. I rolled over and pretended it didn't happen. He tossed and turned all night, ensuring that I stayed awake with every shake of the mattress. There was no sleep sex, but there was no sleep for either of us.

3. Overzealous Cuddling

I decided that the caffeine dose in his steak was too high the previous night, so instead, the next night I opted for normal jammies and just tied the waistband really tight, and no caffeine. I lay facing him with the lights still blazing. I rubbed my fingers through the hair on his chest and tickled him. He was still awake at this point and interested in whatever he was reading by Malcolm

Gladwell. He gently moved my hand to the bed, patting it affectionately. I pressed my body against his, warming his entire side with my cold body, squeezing him like I was Jonas, with the full weight of my body behind it. In response, he shifted away. He tucked some sheets between us and continued reading. I concentrated on my breathing. Soon I was asleep. I slept through the night unmolested as far as I know. I woke up inexplicably cranky.

Lesson Learned: Sometimes you need to adopt the sleep persona of one of the other sleepers to get the restful sleep you deserve.

Chapter 3

Living Through a Man Cold

Candace: Miriam, I need your chicken soup recipe. Paul has a cold.

Miriam: Ok, I will find it and email you.

Candace: Right now. I can't go home without it.

Lucy: I am surprised he let you come out with us.

Candace: There was no "let". He thinks this is a book tour meeting that I couldn't get out of.

Me: You had to lie to your husband in order to get out of the house because he has a cold. How bad is this cold?

Lucy: It is a man cold.

Candace: The man thinks he is dying and he needs me there to watch him do it.

Miriam: Sent.

Me: Do we get days off when we are sick?

Lucy: Not from my family.

Miriam: I am very productive when I am sick. I get the laundry done and usually make soup from scratch because it relaxes me.

Candace: I once had the shits so bad that every time I moved, I had to go. And I still had to play dolls with Karin between shitting. She followed me into the bathroom.

Me: Then why do they get special treatment?

Lucy: Because of the whining. I hate the whining.

Miriam: Bob tries to do things when he is sick, but he ends up doing them so poorly that it is cheaper if he just stays in bed. Last time he had the flu, he broke the light fixture in my living room.

Lucy: Jonas gets the bed to himself so that I am not infected. I give him a bell to summon me with. Although at about day two, I want to shove the bell down his throat.

Me: This could be another opportunity for us.

Candace: Because the last one went so so well.

Me: We could treat them like they treat us when we are sick.

Miriam: Why can't we treat them how we want them to treat us when we are sick?

Candace: Or we can get ourselves sick and treat them like they treat us when they are sick.

Lucy: Oh, the whining.

Really, this was going to go as Candace wanted it to because, so far, her husband was the only one suffering from the man cold. At work, Candace printed out the recipe. On her way home, she stopped at the store for ingredients. She carried them into the house in two giant paper bags. Paul hadn't moved since she left him that morning. She set the bags on the counter before fussing over Paul on the couch. She pressed a hand to his forehead like she would for one of her children. This was a mistake because she had to lean down to touch him and in doing so she got a whiff of sick man smell. You know the smell: part salty armpit sweat, part cat burp, part old shaggy goat. "Phew, Paul. Maybe you should take a bath."

He rolled his head over the back of the sofa to look at her weakly. "I don't think I can get up the stairs for a bath," he said in a soft phlegmy voice.

Poor Paul. He didn't know it but, this was the voice guaranteed to raise Candace's hackles, like fingernails on a chalkboard. She closed her eyes to count in her head backward from ten in Spanish. When she finished with Uno, she opened her eyes, plastered a cheery smile on her lips and said, "C'mon Paul, you will feel better." She took a deep breath of unpolluted oxygen before leaning in again to leverage his arms around her shoulders. Grunting, she leaned backward, using the leverage from her lower body to peel him upward from the couch.

The couch put up a good fight. "I don't even like baths," Paul whisper croaked, sending shudders of distaste down Candace's spine.

"A shower then," she grit through her teeth. "Paul you stink."

He was no help with putting weight on his own two feet. She lost her grip under his arms and he slipped backward to slam his head against the backrest of the couch. "Ow. You don't have to be so mean." He rubbed the back of his head. She noted that he had not lost motor skills in his arms, just his legs. She watched in amazed horror as he dug around in the couch cushion beneath his butt, then brandished the remote triumphantly.

Candace stomped into the kitchen. She began to rustle in the bag of her groceries for vegetables. She pulled out a cutting board and slapped it onto the marble countertop. She had to flip the dial on the gas stove top twice because the first time, her angry movement didn't successfully light the pilot. As much as Paul was annoying her right now, she didn't actually want to burn her house down. After chopping furiously, she threw the vegetables into the metal pot, allowing them to bang satisfyingly. "Could you keep it down? I can't hear the tv," Paul called, risking death or dismemberment by vegetable.

With shaking hands, she slammed the knife flat onto the cutting board, tears from the onions she just chopped welling in her eyes. Grabbing a dish towel to wipe her hands on, she picked up her phone to text Lucy for back up. He was once her brother; she could come and deal with him. Piercing the veil of purple rage came the click clack of plastic heels over the parquet floor, announcing the arrival of Harriet. "Wanna play dress up Mommy?" she asked sweetly.

Candace pressed send on the four-letter word she managed to text to Lucy. In her calm mommy voice, Candace said to her daughter, "You know what honey, Mommy is cooking soup right now, but Daddy is on the couch doing nothing. I am sure he would love to play with you."

Harriet's eyes lit up. She gallop-clicked over to the couch, trailing a rainbow false feather boa with her. "Daddy?" Candace began to chop more sedately now. Paul, who was flipping channels idly, stopped to regard his very pink daughter. "Will you play dress up wif me?"

"Honey, I am too sick right now," he answered in a gravelly voice.

Great big tears welled up in her eyes. "Are you going to heaven?"

Paul leaned forward from the couch to pull his daughter into his lap. He tucked a hand under her chin so that she tilted her head back to look him in the eye. "Honey, why would you ask that?"

"Gretchen's mom got sick and couldn't get up off of the couch to play wif her. Then she went to heaven." Harriet blinked calmly.

Candace rummaged in the cupboard for some dried spices to muffle her laughter.

"Not everyone who gets sick goes to heaven," Paul explained.

"So you're going to hell?" Harriet asked.

"I am not dying," Paul wailed. "Candace," he looked to his wife for aid.

"If you're not dying, maybe your daughter can dress you up while you sit on the couch," she offered instead.

He glared at her. In silent response, she blinked just as sweetly as Harriet until he sighed, defeated.

***

Bob found Miriam vomiting into a toilet one morning. Morning sickness because of the whole pregnancy thing. Bob has a sympathy gag reflex. Before either of them knew it, Miriam had two toilets, a spot on the carpet, and a dog to wash through her morning sickness. "I am really sorry, honey," Bob said, wiping his face with toilet paper.

"Yeah," said Miriam.

Bob cleaned himself up and left for work, leaving Miriam to chase the dog away from the vomit pile her son was scooping up with his sand shovel. She shared her woe with us girls later over text.

Miriam: I couldn't even get him to change a diaper last time, his gag reflex is so high.

Me: Expose him to gag inducing things for an extended period of time so that he develops a tolerance before the baby comes.

Candace: I don't think her carpets can handle that much vomit.

Lucy: Then she should guilt him into getting her the new wood floors she's been wanting.

Candace: Get a dog to clean up baby and husband vomit.

Miriam: I already have one. I had to clean Jimmy this morning.

Me: Who names a dog Jimmy?

Lucy: Get a cat to clean the dog.

Miriam: Jimmy is named after Jimmy Carter.

Candace: Ok. Nevermind. I am for the guilt floors.

Miriam: How did Paul like the soup?

Paul did not like the soup. He convinced his son Joey to put his sister to bed with the bribe of a new app for his phone, then flopped backward onto the couch just as the soup timer rang.

His loving wife served him the warm soup on the couch while he cuddled up beneath a warm blanket. Eating on the couch was something he knew his wife abhorred the children doing. He was grateful to be an adult. The aromas floated up from the steaming liquid in the soup bowl. The steam cloud was a visible pair of hands cupping his face in a warm hug. He breathed the steam into his lungs with a sigh.

Candace had set up her own plate and dish at the table in the kitchen, ostensibly to avoid contamination. He dished the broth onto his spoon, blew on it and inserted the delectable cure-all Bob raved about into his mouth. Immediately, Paul recognized his error. The liquid scalded his delicate tongue, then proceeded to coat the whole inside of his mouth with an inferno. Reflexively, he opened his mouth to expel the heat and some of the liquid fire dribbled down his shirt front. Once the immediate threat was removed, however, the secondary attack revealed itself to his sinuses. The fires of hell rose into his sinus, riding his nerve endings all the way into his eyeballs. Tears as large as Harriet's pooled. He was now afraid that if he allowed them to fall onto his cheeks, they would feel like acid melting his cheeks. Snot began to run down his nose in rivulets too fast to catch with a shirt sleeve before reaching the top of his lip.

"Dear god," he choked out. "What is this?"

He heard the chink of spoon on saucer from behind the couch. "White habanero pepper really clears the sinuses, according to Miriam." She said sweetly. "Is it too much?"

Paul was sure he would have third-degree burns from his snot tomorrow on his face.

Candace was sure he was going back to work tomorrow, but just to make sure, "I'll save it for lunch tomorrow too."

***

As Bob vomited for the second time that week into the houseplant to avoid the carpet, Miriam brought him a cold compress for his head. "I am sorry," he mumbled beneath the fabric.

Miriam knew this was the moment she had been waiting for. "How sorry?"

Savoring the cool feel of towel to forehead, Bob backed away from the smell of vomit remaining in the houseplant so quickly that he collided with his wife. She fell to her bottom with an expelled "oof". Horrified at his clumsiness, he helped her to her feet, dropping his towel in order to pat her down for injuries. She swatted his hands away, making directly for the plant. He knew it was too heavy for her to lift on her own. He wasn't sure how she'd managed to clean it after the last time. He bent to help her lift it when the smell assailed him again. His knees buckled, crumpling him to the floor in her path.

Letting go of the molested plant, Miriam sighed and put a hand to her lower back to stretch out the aches that had settled permanently there. "I am replacing the floors, Bob."

He rubbed his fingers through the stiff brown strands of carpet where he sat, perplexed by her non linear train of thought. "How does vomit in the houseplant lead to you getting new floors?"

"It's not just in the houseplant, Bob." She crossed her arms over her plump chest.

"Stop saying my name like that." He said from his position on the floor.

"Like what, Bob?"

"Like I am a recalcitrant child that you need to remind to use his manners."

"You haven't changed a single diaper since John was born." She raised an eyebrow, challenging him to deny it.

"I didn't want to puke on the kid. And what does that have to do with anything else?"

She rubbed her prematurely bulging belly. "I don't know if you've noticed, but there's about to be another person in this house, Bob. And babies puke. A lot." She nudged him with her foot. "Especially your babies."

He caught a hold of her dress and pulled her down to the floor with him so he could stroke the belly. She was always nicer when he stroked her belly. "And I bought you a carpet shampooer for Christmas."

She picked up his hand and pulled it away from her belly and placed it further north. "A carpet cleaner is not as effective as a mop."

He nuzzled her neck with his nose. "But the cleaner was $600. And you have barely used it."

She backed up so quickly that it propelled him forward headfirst into the carpet. She stood up and began to lug the plant toward the garage. "I am carrying your child for the second time, Bob. You do remember what happened last time."

He did remember. He still had nightmares about it. Why were men encouraged to be in the room these days? She'd almost bled out in an elevator on the way up to the special birthing suite, screaming all sorts of obscenities at him as he pulled a leg up to her forehead. "That argument isn't going to work forever, you know."

Miriam smiled smugly. "Yes it will."

***

Paul did, in fact, return to work feeling remarkably better. His face still itched from the calamine lotion he'd applied after the soup incident, but at least he was free from Harriet's worried ministrations. He could always shut his office door if he started to feel miserable again.

He picked up his phone to a sobbing man. "She's left me and taken the kids," said the raspy voice.

"Who is this?" Paul asked.

"Your brother-in-law." The man, Jonas, sobbed so loudly that Paul had to pull the phone away from his ear.

Paul couldn't say that he was surprised. Lucy, after all, has always been a free spirit. Jonas was obviously not man enough to tame her. "What happened?" he asked when what he was really wondering was if there would be an extra family invading his home. He fished in his drawer for his cellphone to text Candace.

"She – she said that I should rest up and she would take the kids on an adventure so I can sleep and get over this cold. "Paul, drumming his fingers on his desk, stopped, confused. Luckily, he didn't have to say anything to encourage Jonas to spill more details. "They went camping without me. How could she? That's my thing."

Paul frowned at the phone. Jonas' tirade had been reduced to crying and sniffling. "Jonas." Paul called, hoping the man didn't choke on his own muck. "Did she leave you some soup?"

"Miriam's soup, yeah. But who is going to heat it up for me?"

***

I opened the door to my bedroom slowly, allowing the hallway light to illuminate me like a spotlight on a dark stage. Clifford watched from his pile of pillows on the bed, attempting to stifle a sneeze with his elbow. Sexily, I adjusted the face mask over my nose with a gloved hand. "This is only going to hurt a little," I said, approaching the bed. A negligee draped down one of my shoulders, revealing a creamy, bare globe.

Lucy: You did not!

Me: Of course I did.

Candace: Why risk getting sick yourself?

Me: I was wearing PPE. Besides, it has been scientifically proven that moving the lymph around heals a sickness faster.

Candace: Jenna, moving the lymph around?

Me: Exercise

Lucy: Then make him go for a walk.

Me: You try getting Clifford to exercise.

Miriam: No thanks.

Lesson Learned: Miriam's White Habanero Pepper Chicken Tortilla Soup really can cure a man cold. See Recipe at the back of the book.

Chapter 4

You Are Not a Child. You Should Not Cook Like One.

Miriam requires Bob to cook at least once in a seven-day period. When asked about this requirement, she said that she didn't want him to ever forget how. Personally, I think the woman is a saint for allowing him into the kitchen.

For reference, here is how Miriam cooks.

Miriam opened the refrigerator at 2pm. She looked at the contents. She asked herself, what is likely to go bad if not eaten? If they had leftovers, what would make a better lunch than dinner? She next checked the contents of her pantry of dried non-perishable foods and began to develop a plan for what could go together to make a meal. She followed up her plan by making a list of items she might need from the store. She added to the list any items she noted were low in their general supplies.

She packed up the toddler for a store trip. At the store, she purchased only items from her list. She used coupons she stored in her wallet from things she normally purchased.

Once home, she put away her groceries. She then emptied the dishwasher.

At 430pm she chopped the vegetables into colorful segmented piles, leaving them on a cutting board for later addition to the sauce she would make. She opened the refrigerator, took out a stick of butter, cut off a sliver into a pan, then replaced the rest of the bar in the refrigerator on its original shelf.

She opened the package of meat, placed the meat on top of the now melted butter in the pan, then discarded the wrapper in the garbage can. She carried the vegetables to the pan on the cutting board, rolling the thick plastic up to allow them to drop into the pan without spilling. She placed the knife and cutting board into the sink for washing.

She chose a spice container from her alphabetized spice shelf, added a dash to the pan, then flipped the contents around with a spatula. She set the spatula down on a spill plate, allowing the food to sizzle and crisp. She put the spice container back into its spot on the shelf.

She placed the water for her dinner starch side-dish on the burner to boil, adding a little salt from the kitchen salt shaker she left in the middle of the kitchen table for this purpose. She put the salt shaker back in its spot, then added the starch to the boiling water. She pulled a colander out of its cupboard to place in the sink for draining. She finished the meat by stirring once, then turning the burner off and covering it.

Pulling out plates for each member of her family, she set them on the counter beside the burners. She plated a portion onto each plate that was appropriate to that individual's appetite. She assigned Bob to get the drinks, napkins, and silverware to set the table. While Bob was setting the table, she rinsed the pans, colander, and cutting board and placed them into the dishwasher.

Her food is always amazing.

***

For comparison, how Bob cooks.

It was 530 when Bob remembered that it was his night to cook. He opened the app Miriam downloaded onto his iPhone and entered the ingredients he found in the refrigerator. A recipe populated the screen, but he didn't like the look of it, so he skimmed through a list until he found something that looked easy to make.

He opened a can, then remembered that he had to boil some water. He started the burner for the water, filled the pot, and sloshed the water onto the burner with a satisfying sizzle. He pulled out another pan to pour the contents of the can into. He realized after pouring half of the can into the chosen pan that it was too small for the rest of the recipe. He pulled out a larger pan, then dribbled the contents into the new pan. Using a spatula, he scraped every last drop from the can and small pan. Both spatula and small pan were placed next to the sink for washing.

He pulled 5 different spices he thought he might need from Miriam's spice shelf, setting them out on the counter in no particular order. He added a lot of spice. Maybe too much. He grabbed a spoon out of the drawer to scoop some of the spice off of the top. He mixed the rest in, then tasted his concoction. After he added more spice, he got a new spoon to taste that. Satisfied, all three spoons rested on the counter.

His starch boiled over. He picked the pot off the burner without turning the burner off. The handles were wicked hot and he dropped the whole thing on to the sink. He pulled the colander out of the cabinet. Then remembered that he should probably have used a hot pad. He opened multiple drawers, looking for hot pads. Ramming his side into an opened drawer, he grunted. He found them finally resting on the clean dish side of the sink out in the open. He also found appetizer crackers.

He pulled out plates for his family, placing the half-eaten bag of crackers onto his son's plate. The starch and canned something or other were plated. He observed that there was a large amount of white space left over on the plates. He thought that they looked too empty. He pulled a vegetable out of the fridge and the butter. He grabbed another pan and a cutting board. Slicing a piece of butter into the pan, he left the rest of the butter on the countertop near the dirty spoons. Realizing that he ran out of counter space, he chopped the vegetable in the open space near the clean dishes. He scooped the chopped vegetables into his hands to be carried to the pan with the melted butter. Some pieces of the vegetables didn't make it. He grabbed a new spatula to mix the veggies.

By this time, the stuff already on the plates had congealed. He pulled out a fresh pan to reheat the plate contents, cursing their lack of microwave. Miriam got rid of it mid pregnancy when she was reading about gamma rays.

Everything was plated and ready by 645. Miriam turned off the burner at 646.

She pat him on the arm, said thank- you, and agreed to wash the dishes if he would put the kid to bed.

Bob is an excellent cook compared to my husband.

***

Me: My husband is a child.
Candace: They all are.
Lucy: What did he do?
Me: He can't cook grown up food.

I tell them the story of the night before.

At 430pm Clifford texted me, "What's for dinner?"
I didn't answer because I was teaching a class.
At 435pm he sent another text. "You said something about fish tacos this morning and I am passing the store on my way home so I could get that if that is still what you want."
I was still in class.
He drove past the store all the way home. He greeted the kids.
He asked them, "What shall Daddy make for dinner?"
"Cookies!" my daughter shouted gleefully.
"Chocolate pancakes," my son responded, just as hopefully.
Clifford shrugged, considering the parenting advice he received from sage parenting expert Bill Cosby from the 1970s "If it has milk and eggs and flour it must be healthy."
He rubbed his hands together happily. He cooked the pancakes, flipping them perfectly in the pan. The mixing bowl rested precariously on the sink, unrinsed. The pan left on the burner, in case the kids wanted more.

At 530pm he sent me another text, "Kids and I have eaten, you should probably pick up something on your own on your way home."

I stopped at the martini bar on the way home. When I finally walked in the door at 7pm, I found the three of them snuggled up on the couch watching Captain Underpants. The kids' homework hadn't been checked. The dishes hadn't been done. Stephen had chocolate in his hair, at least I hoped it was chocolate.

My son greeted me with, "Hi mom. I am hungry, what's for dinner?"

Candace: The answer to your problems is meal planning.

Me: With what time?

Miriam: Do you want to eat kid food forever?

Me: I hate Ramen.

Candace: I make time and I run my own business.

Lucy: Jonas doesn't follow the meal plan I make. He says it stifles his creativity.

For fun, how Jonas cooks.

Jonas looked at the meal plan color coded and taped to their non metallic fronted refrigerator. Jonas did not open the door of the refrigerator. Jonas picked up his cell phone to order takeout online.

Miriam: Following the meal plan can be tough. Sometimes I make Thursday's meal on Tuesday. When I do that, Bob's app can't find anything to make with the leftovers, so we have takeout.

Lucy: You work with students, right?

Me: I am a professor.

Lucy: have them help you set up a timed text to send to Clifford when you know he will be wanting to know what to make for dinner.

Me: Brilliant.

So I try it.

He made Chicken ala King for dinner on his day off. He used every pot and pan we own. It was burned so badly that two of the pans needed to be thrown out because no amount of scraping could get the burn off. The kids refused to eat it. We put them to bed hungry. We did the dishes together. He smiled at me and he scrubbed yet another pot. "I like this meal planning thing."

So long as I am not the only one cleaning up this mess, I like it too.

Lesson Learned: No one can get better at an activity unless we give them an opportunity to practice, fail, and try again. And ordering take out for dinner is a perfectly reasonable option when you don't want to clean the kitchen...again.

Chapter 5

No One LIKES to Do Chores

Lucy: I read an article in the New Yorker that Japanese women do 90% of the household chores.

Me: Who does the other 10%?

Candace: Not my husband.

Miriam: There are certain household tasks, I don't want Bob doing.

Lucy: 90% of them, though?

Me: Early in our marriage, Clifford made a spreadsheet to divide the hours of labor.

Candace: How'd that work out for him?

Me: Not good. His math was off.

Lucy: The real problem is that they choose the wrong stuff to help with.

Miriam (munching a freshly powdered donut): That's what I meant. I don't mind the cooking or the laundry, but I hate taking out the garbage. What does he do? Fold the laundry.

Me: Sweeping the floor when I am clearly trying to cook.

Lucy: Fixing something that doesn't need to be fixed when we are trying to leave the house.

Candace: Teaching me how to do a task better.

We'd decided to shop at a Farmer's market instead of meet for coffee. Something about a health food kick that Lucy was on. It smelled of patchouli, but the berries were fresh and juicy. We laughed about the fact that none of our husbands would have chosen to be there with us. Or even thought of shopping for the family at a farmer's market twenty minutes out of the way of our normal commute.

After Lucy shared her article with me, I started wondering why the division of labor between men and women was so lopsided. Even today, the best statistics estimate that women perform 25 times more household tasks than men. Part of what Miriam hinted at is that there are certain tasks that are linked with our identities as women that we don't want to give over to men. Usually these tasks have to do with child rearing. We start out at home with newborns, alternately recovering from whatever ordeal we had to face in dispelling them from our bodies and translating out their different cries.

While someone has to take on the financial burden of maintaining household income.

What it really comes down to, though, is tolerance. Some people have a different tolerance for how cluttered a space can be. Considerate partners, or partners like my husband who are looking to barter my good favor for sex, will attempt to be cognizant of which chores their partners have the lowest tolerance for and do them quickly. Especially if it is an easy task, the reward can be swift.

I told them about my previous weekend as an example.

Satisfied that every dish from dinner the night before was crammed into the dishwasher, the clothes dryer was running and the kids were snuggled together like puppies on the floor in front of a Barbie movie, I left for a long shower. Long showers are what make the weekend the weekend.

Clifford sprawled facedown on our mattress, his bare arms stretched over both pillows. I bent over to kiss the back of his neck before shutting and locking the bathroom door behind me. I loved how the steam of the shower caressed my bare skin. I closed my eyes to breathe in the heat. I loved Saturdays especially.

When I ran out of body parts to scrub, I reluctantly shut off the shower stream. After dressing, I opened my bedroom door to be knocked backward by the smell of fried butter. Clifford was in the kitchen.

The children had not moved from their tangled floor heap. On the dining table was waiting for me a cup containing a freshly cut flower and a plate of powdered beignets. My whole body smiled after I wolfed them down. I hoped he already ate his share because they were gone in a single inhale.

I took my plate into the kitchen to pour myself some coffee. There I saw it. This was not the same kitchen I had left to shower. An empty powdered sugar bag was balanced on the Keurig. Powdered crumbs coated the sink, the toaster, the counters and stove. Did he get into a fight with the bag? Three different sized mixing bowls rested on their sides next to the sink. The cap was off the milk container, which was still out warming on the counter. I thought to myself, how long was my shower?

I wet a rag to wipe down the poor toaster, who didn't harm anyone, and the coffee pot, because I still wanted to use it. Throwing away some discarded wrappers, I began to grumble. I was putting away the milk container when my daughter Becca entered the kitchen to ask for a cup of milk. I put the milk away again when my son also asked for a cup of milk and cereal.

I let them eat in front of the tv then went hunting for my husband. I found him mowing the lawn wearing a button-up shirt and his Gucci loafers. I shook my head at him. Seeing me, he stalled the mower to lope over and kiss my cheek. "Did you have a delicious breakfast?"

I sighed. What was the point in making him feel bad about the state of the kitchen? I rubbed my belly. "I hope you didn't want any." Then I gave him an up and down appraisal. "What are you wearing?"

He lifted up a muddied expensive shoe. "I was dressed and then I remembered that I needed to mow the lawn." He shrugged. "I didn't want to go back upstairs."

I rolled my eyes, wondering how to clean the grass stains out of Gucci. Maybe there was a YouTube video for that. "What else do you have planned for today?" I asked curiously.

He considered, "A shower, dig some holes, weed the garden, maybe a bike ride."

"Not in that order," I suggested.

"What are you and the kids doing?" he asked. Me and the kids? As if it was a foregone conclusion that I am a unit with the kids on the weekends. That I am their entertainment, while he got the weekend to do whatever he wanted.

This is my fault. This is our weekend ritual. I drive them to playdates, birthday parties, parks, sporting events on the weekends while he works out or works in the yard or works on leftover work from the work week. The idea of so much work exhausts me. However, once, after a particularly grueling day that involved a cross city search for a particular Halloween costume item during which I actually performed the back seat blind alternating child whacking to break up a kid fight, I came home to a quiet house and found him napping. God, I want a nap. I miss when the children would nap and I would snuggle Clifford on our tiny couch and listen to the rise and fall of his chest as he breathed.

We came up with this weekend division of duties to keep me away from household chores like laundry or tinkering in the garden because things often cost more money and time when I do them. And I do like weekend adventuring with my children. I even send Clifford calendar invites to things I expect him to attend. Sometimes he responds "maybe" to my invites to our own home, which he knows makes me laugh. So it is perfectly natural for him to expect that I have made plans for the kids and me without including him. After all, it hasn't made his calendar.

This day I felt like upending the norm. I wanted to tinker in the garden instead of playing hostess to two tiny Napoleans. I blinked at my darling husband. "The kids can fend for themselves today." I said, commandeering a rake. "I am helping you."

He grit his teeth in some semblance of a grimace/ smile. "That's so helpful, honey. They're five and seven now. What could possibly go wrong?"

I chose not to read the sarcasm in his voice, but instead set myself to work. After a few minutes, hours, days of shoveling, I was sweating profusely. I didn't dare look up from my task to see what progress Clifford was making, because then I might actually know how much time had actually passed, and that wouldn't be good for my ego. I slammed the shovel yet again into the dirt mound that was no deeper than my shoe and the damn shovel bent.

At that moment, the back door creaked open. Steven poked his head out. "Mom, can we make ice cream?"

"Make ice cream?"

"Becca found a recipe online."

The chunk of dirt I was wrestling with finally gave way, sending all of my force downward with no opposition. I sprawled face down right onto the shovel. None of my family members attempted to help me up. Clearly, they were aware that this wasn't the first time I had tripped over a garden tool. From my vantage in the dirt, I mulled over the request. "Well, your father already destroyed the kitchen," I grumbled.

Before I could say anything more, Steven whooped with delight and pulled his whole body back through the door. "She said yes," I heard him shout inside to his sister somewhere. I didn't actually, but my lack of an immediate no answer was seized upon by an opportunistic child. They know me so well. I rolled my eyes, pulled myself up, and began digging with renewed vigor.

When I fell for the second time, I took a moment to observe the green of the grass and the absolute peace and quiet that was my backyard. It was too quiet. Looking around, I realized that I was the only one still digging; Clifford was gone. Feeling betrayed, after all this was his project, I dusted myself off a second time, jammed the shovel into the dirt, and peeked over the back fence. There I found him chatting animatedly with a neighbor. I cleared my throat, making him turn. His jaw quivered into a sheepish grin. "I was getting the mail," he explained.

I wiped a smudge of dirt from my cheek, which ended up smearing it all the way to my ear. "I see." Withdrawing my head from the fence line, I left him to finish whatever deep HOA discussion they were clearly having.

By the time he reappeared, it was to find me sprawled out with my feet up on our winterized outdoor chairs, book in hand, shovel abandoned beneath the spider webbed swing set.

"Where are the kids?" Over the years, this has become part of our language, like we have a secret code only other married couples understand. We never call each other by our names, only "hon" or "sweetheart", which conveys more about how we are feeling about the person at the moment, than an emphasis on a name could. We never said hello, instead it's "where are the kids?" or "how are the kids?" or "have you seen the kids?". My favorite of our codes is "We have to let the dog out" which is code for "It is time to leave this boring event". It is code because we don't actually have a dog.

I shrugged as if I couldn't care less about where the actual kids were. The truth was that I was afraid to go inside the house. I didn't know what kind of damage they had inflicted on each other, or worse, the house, since we had been out here. I fully realized that it was my choice to leave them unsupervised with access to the kitchen and the internet. I was just not mentally prepared to face up to whatever the consequences of that choice may lie at my feet. I knew that by making that choice, I would have to clean it up. Whatever it turned out to be. I shuddered at the possibilities.

Probably feeling the same anxiety, he sat in the chair across from me and pulled my feet into his lap. "Thanks for the help today," he said, idly rubbing my dirt crusted socked feet.

I peeked over my book to observe the unfilled holes in our grass. "Why are we digging holes again?"

"To aerate the grass." As if I understand the purpose of that.

"Clifford," I said, "I hate yard work."

"I know," he grinned knowingly. "But do you like any of the adulting we do on the weekends?"

I considered. My hands had fresh blisters. My feet felt crusty. My kitchen was probably sticky and smelled of spoiled milk at the moment. I considered how much it would cost to hire any of these activities out. "Not really." I knew I was going to have to go inside and face the kitchen, because of the two evils, a milky smelling kitchen beat out being defeated by a shovel. "What else are you doing out here?" I asked hopefully, stalling.

"Testing the sprinkler system." I loved this man for throwing me something I could finally work with.

With a zip, I pulled my feet from his lap. I gathered up the strength I needed to saunter saucily into the house. "I'll make lunch for you when you get done with that," I tossed out over my shoulder.

When I entered the kitchen, I was greeted with the sight of rainbow colored bowls upended, dripping their contents into the carpet. The powdered sugar was coating the counters again and there were child sized footprints in it, both on the counters and on the floor. I knew I had two choices in that moment 1) I could make my children clean up through a carefully calibrated argument and bribery system which would either teach them a valuable life lesson about contributing to the household or piss them off, or 2) I could inspire them to annoy their father. The decision was made before I came in here. "Kids, Daddy's turning the sprinklers on."

"Yay!" they shouted in synchrony, running down the hall stripping clothes, abandoning them like lost detritus on the way.

"Pick those up and put them in your hampers," I hollered. Laundry. Check. Once they were outside in the sprinklers, the bath would be complete. Check. Check. I was rocking this chores thing.

I dug up a mop from the back of the pantry, thinking of the choice the 1950s mom would have made. When it was sunny outside, she didn't have her children doing chores. She sent them off to the woods somewhere to be imaginative children so she could complete her housework in peace. She didn't see them again until dark after she had had a couple of martinis with her friends. Which reminded me that I should probably go to the store and pick up some martini mix.

Lucy: So you tried his chores and realized they weren't for you?

Miriam: The grass is always greener.

Candace: How pissed was he that he had the kids "helping" with the sprinklers?

Me: About as pissed as I was cleaning the kitchen for the third time.

Lucy: He could have cleaned the kitchen. I thought that was what this was all about?

Candace: No. He would put things in the wrong cabinets and she would never find them again.

Miriam: She appreciated cleaning the kitchen more after digging the holes.

Candace: I wish Paul could appreciate something.

Me: Sometimes the lesson being learned has to be me learning it.

Lucy making a gagging noise

Miriam: That is so profound.

Later that evening...

Candace arrived home exhausted from work at 5:07 pm, which was just enough time to get Harriet into her ballet outfit and drop her off before she had to pick up Joey from debate practice. She unlocked the door to usher Harriet inside, giving her one last warning to hurry or they'd be late again. When she crossed the threshold into the bright cheery kitchen, smells of basil, garlic and sausage assailed her senses. This was unexpected. Cursory observation of this mysterious happening revealed pots boiling, sausage sizzling, cutting board messily filled with chopped greenery, a mountain of dirtied copper-bottomed pots that are impossible to clean because they aren't dishwasher safe, and Paul. "Welcome home, honey," he said with a beatific smile gracing his chiseled face.

Now here is how Paul expected her to answer. "Paul? You did all of this?" He nodded. "I've never loved you more than right now." Then she threw herself into his arms. The whisk he was holding clattered out of his hands as he rushed to catch her up in a romantic embrace. Sappy music swelled. She whispered into his neck, "Take me upstairs. The food can wait."

Here is what she actually said, "Paul, you did all of this?" He nodded. "Do you have any idea whatsoever goes on in this house?" He gulped. "It is Tuesday which means I have exactly," she consulted the watch on her left wrist, "thirty-five minutes to dump Harriet off at ballet, pick up Joey from debate at the highschool to drop him off at piano, to drive back here in time to meet Karin's soccer coach who has generously agreed to drop her off here every other Tuesday, so that I have time to pick Harriet up from ballet then Joey from piano. It is not dinner time." During the entirety of her tirade, she looped the kitchen frantically, snatching up open wrappers that littered the counter top. He was still brandishing a whisk graced by spaghetti sauce protectively in front of him. She brushed too close to him in her frantic cleaning and, of course, the white blouse she was wearing was painted with sauce.

She glared down at it as if it were a life ending saber strike.

Harriet thundered down the stairs. "Mommy, I am ready."

With a groaning glance at the dishes she would be washing by hand later this evening, Candace ushered her daughter out of the house, still wearing part of dinner, two minutes behind schedule.

***

In another part of town, my story actually inspired Lucy to encourage a little change in her household ...

After yet another 45 minute pooping session, Jonas exited the downstairs guest bathroom and nearly fell on his face into the kitchen over the plastic bag lying in wait for him. "Lucy, why is there a garbage bag waiting for me outside of the bathroom door?"

After meeting us at the Farmer's Market, she had a pot of something organic simmering on the stove and she was "watching it" by flipping through a workout magazine while hovering over the kitchen counter. "I am sure you are smart enough to figure it out on your own, without me telling you," she answered.

"Isn't this why we had children? So they could do these chores?" he grumbled to his wife, hefting the bag onto his shoulder.

Sighing, she explained, "They are six, Jonas. They can barely tie their own shoes." Both parents looked at the recent product of artwork that had come home from school currently displayed on the refrigerator. Danielle's was a mishmash of jagged recyclables glued to a piece of frayed cardboard cereal box. Emily's picture was painted on a droopy, flimsy paper substance, the picture resembling a dog or cat of some sort, covered in a mixture of colors that should have probably never been on the same page together. "We can't expect them to do chores without hurting themselves."

Undeterred, Jonas lowered the garbage bag from his shoulder, hovering it above the ground by his hand as if testing its weight. "There's not much to this. I think it is time they learned."

Lucy waved a hand in the air graciously. "Then you, as their caring, involved father, should teach them."

He glared at her, wondering what kind of trap she was leading him into. Unable to figure it out, he carefully balanced the bag against the island, taking up the center of their kitchen before opening the door to the basement in search of his proteges. Pasting a cheerful smile on his face, he hollered, "Girls!"

No answer.

Sighing, because he knew he would have to enter their domain, he steeled himself for what he would find. As he rounded the dog-leg of the stairs, he spotted them. Danielle was perched on a chair attempting to place an old shoebox on top of a tower about 60 inches off of the ground, that she'd obviously constructed out of pilfered garbage. She was wearing an orange home depot apron, safety glasses on top of her head, and over that, an extra large white lab coat- god only knows where she'd found that. He thought she looked like a mad scientist. In contrast, sweet Emily was stomach down on the floor, in tumbling range of her twin's monstrous structure, play-acting naked Barbie dolls kissing. She was wearing red sparkly shoes kicked up in the air behind her, a flower girl dress that was partially undone over unicorn footie pajamas.

Jonas, feeling so much love for his daughters and their unique selves in that moment, took the stance of a spunky camp counselor. "Girls, want to help Daddy with something?"

Emily answered first. "Not right now, Daddy." She laid her Barbie doll on the ground, then nestled Ken right next to her under a blanket. Without warning, Danielle leaped back from her creation, brushing a precariously balanced piece with her elbow. The monstrous tower crumbled on top of Emily and her dolls, burying her in rubble. Both girls screamed so loud that it echoed inside Jonas' head.

"Daddy," Danielle scolded, "You toppled my master-piece."

Jonas bent to pick up one of the boxes now resting at his feet. He quickly deconstructed it into a flat piece of cardboard while his daughter watched on in horror. "That was mine," she shrieked.

"That was recycling." Jonas explained. "We recycle cardboard in this house."

Danielle began frantically scooping the other boxes away from her father. "Well, I am recycling them into art." Her new pile of boxes tumbled over on top of Emily again, who shouted at her sister before diving beneath the pile for her dolls. She resurfaced with the dolls and a crumple of bubble wrap, looking victorious. She kissed both dolls before rolling them up in the bubble wrap and setting them in a bed obviously made from a discarded shoebox.

Jonas glared at the box. He wasn't aware that his wife shopped at that particularly expensive store.

"Are you here to play with us, Daddy?" Emily asked.

Jonas felt the noose tighten. "Umm. How about we play your game after we do one tiny thing with Daddy?"

Danielle looked up from examining the flattened cardboard she had snatched back from him. "What's that Daddy?"

He plastered his best this-will-be-super-fun-I'm-not-lying face on and said, "We are going to take out all of the garbages."

"Ew." Emily said.

"Why do we have to do that?" Danielle asked.

"Well, your mother and I thought it was time for you to learn how to do some chores."

"I'll cook dinner," Emily offered.

"I'll sweep the floor," said Danielle.

"What?" Jonas asked. He couldn't imagine that his daughters actually knew how to do those tasks if they didn't even know how to take out the garbage. Then again, his wife didn't really know how to do the garbage, otherwise she wouldn't be making him do it. "No, we are taking out the garbage because it needs to be done."

Somehow, that convinced them to at least follow him out of the basement. As they returned to where he had left the bag, he saw that he had taken too long. Their golden retriever, Pokey, had found it first. His head was buried in some delicious red substance that might have been a meat wrapper. Sensing their approach, the dog lifted his garish head in a large, wet doggy smile. The girls screamed again.

"Is everything ok?" Lucy called from somewhere else in the house, probably her workout room, he thought bitterly. Determined to see this through, he shushed the girls, then shooed the dog away from the mess. He herded the beast into their downstairs bedroom, momentarily admired his wife's bent over figure, then locked the dog in with her. He chuckled at a muffled squeal as the dog found his next victim.

He caught up with the girls trying to sneak back down to their lair. "Emily, I need you to follow me into the kitchen to get supplies to clean this up." She nodded her agreement glumly.

Danielle patted her arm comfortingly. "Don't worry, I have some rubber gloves I have been saving. I will get them for you." Sometimes his daughter's ingenuity terrified him.

New garbage bag, gloves and bleach wipes acquired, Jonas and his daughters reconvened once again in the hallway between the kitchen and basement. They found the dog back at it. "Danielle, did you let Pokey out?"

She tugged on her blue rubber gloves, gleefully snapping them finger by finger. "No, he got out when I got the gloves from under your sink." She turned to her sister, waving an extra pair in Emily's face. "Want some?"

Emily jutted a big lip outward and shook her head vehemently. "Daddy, I don't want to do this."

"Well honey, doing chores helps us all and makes you a valuable member of the household." Jonas said.

Emily sucked in a deep, hiccupping breath, allowing a fat tear to streak its way down her round cheek. "You don't think I am valuable?"

"I didn't say that." Jonas back pedaled while wrestling the dog back toward his room. "It is just that some day me and mommy won't be here to help you with these things."

"You're dying?" Emily wailed, clutching at her sister for moral support.

Dog deposited, Jonas bent down to scoop items into his new bag. "I am not dying," he grunted. "Just help me scoop." He sent a pained look to Danielle. "Quit stalling. You could have been done with this already."

Danielle removed her sister's clutching embrace and bent down to pick up an item. She stopped, looked at it, then set it aside. She picked up another item. Inspired by her sister's bravery in the face of yucky things, Emily crouched down as well and scooped handfuls of items toward her father's feet. Encouraged by their efforts, Jonas held open the bag happily to claim Emily's increasingly eager scoops. Jonas signaled Emily to pause so he could shift the contents of the bag. She watched her sister's slow, careful examination of yet another item. "What are you doing?"

"Saving building supplies," Danielle answered curtly, shoveling her finds into the hem of her shirt. Jonas decided now was not the time to protest, considering that one of his offspring had proven helpful. Seeing that Danielle had laid claim to the rest of the unchewed items on their floor, Jonas pulled the drawstring of the bag tight. Smarter and wiser now, he carried the full bag with him as he shuffled the girls upstairs to empty the bathroom garbage.

"Daddy, will you carry me?" Emily begged halfway up the stairs. He could have sworn he heard his wife's phantom chuckle, but the sound was so brief he couldn't be sure.

"No, I can't carry you. I am carrying the bag."

"You have a second hand," Danielle helpfully pointed out.

"That hand is going to carry the second bag."

"Then what do you need us for?" Emily asked.

Jonas sighed. "To open the door."

Once the bathroom garbage was successfully bagged, the troops were ushered back down the stairs. Jonas balanced the new bag between the two gloved girls so he could open the front door. They groaned and grunted as they heaved their load to the outside garbage can. Danielle balanced the bag on her sister's head to leverage it into the can. It teetered, fell and spilled the contents into the street. Emily started crying again, and the dog came out of the still open door to lick up her tears and the fresh garbage. This didn't seem worth it anymore.

* * *

And even later in the evening, Candace was loading the dishwasher while Paul made sure Karin didn't drown in the bathtub, aka playing on his work phone outside the bathroom door. She decided that his spaghetti was spectacular even after reheating. When he came down to help her load, she asked, "Where'd you learn to cook like that?"

Now here was how Candace expected him to answer. "You taught me." He strokes a hand down her slightly dampened apron. "Watching you every day inspired me to do something just for you. You amaze me." Then he swept her up into his strong manly surgeon arms. The dish towel she was holding plops into the sudsy sink.

Sappy music swells. She whispers into his neck, "Take me upstairs. The rest can wait."

Instead of answering, he pulled a dish that she had just placed into the dishwasher out, considered the spacing, then put it back in at a different angle. She stopped what she was doing in order to watch him repeat the action with a second and third dish, then pull a fourth dish out altogether, to set it on the side of the counter with the clean hand dried dishes. "Didn't you read the manual on this thing when we bought it?" he grumbled after becoming aware of her observation.

She blinked at him uncomprehendingly, dish-towel tucked under her crossed arms. "No, who does that?"

"I do," he replied, not pulling his eyes away from his engineering task. "And it said that circular orientation was most efficient for a thorough clean in this device."

"Well, circular orientation won't fit all of the dishes that need washing," she explained, taking in the almost bare counter and the straining dishwasher. It was as if he had no comprehension of how long she had been scrubbing these damn dishes.

He shrugged. "Then we can do two loads." He reached down to reorient another bowl.

She slapped the damp dish towel she was holding into the soapy, half cleared sink. The soap slopped satisfyingly over the edge and dribbled to the floor. "Fine. Great. It has been decreed. This is now your chore." She turned on a heel toward the stairs to her room.

"You're a real piece of work, you know that." His gravely voice shivered down her spine with foreboding. She shut her eyes, counted her breaths, made an attempt to remain Zen. It didn't help. He was six inches from her face when she opened her eyes. That was too much in her space. She had to step back. She hated stepping back. "I got no thank you for the meal. I came home from work early to make you."

Candace narrowed her brow, then stepped closer to him. He didn't step back and that irritated her, too. "I get no thank you every damn day for all of the shit I do around here, and you expect a thank you for one goddamned meal?" She pointedly glanced at the ceiling above the stove. "You got sauce on the ceiling."

He looked up. Sure enough, red splatters marred the pure white crown molding. He puffed out his cheeks, chagrined. "I just wanted to do something nice."

The food had been nice, but it just made more work for her in the end. She didn't like his version of nice. "You want to do something nice? Clean up your own damned mess." At that, Candace made her escape.

Lesson Learned: It takes creativity to delegate chores and sometimes it is not worth it.

Chapter 6

How to End an Argument

Candace: I think for the health and wellbeing of my children I need to surrender The Dish War.

Lucy (kinda pirratey): Never surrender. He will only see it as weakness.

Miriam: He isn't eating at home most nights, anyway. So you and the kids are the only ones suffering from this.

Me: You could do it so poorly that he is driven to fix it.

Candace: I don't think I can do that.

Lucy: How would that even work?

So I give them the example of a classic morning in my house.

I was sorting my papers for class in my bathrobe when Clifford bellowed incoherently from the bedroom. "I cannot hear you when you bellow from the bedroom." I shouted back.

He came out pants-less with a purple shirt half buttoned and a tie dangling untied around his shoulders. "What did you say?"

I smiled. "What did you ask while in there?"

"Touche." He acknowledged. "Where is my belt?"

I set down my papers to retie my robe. "Where did you see it last?"

He put his hands on his hips sternly. I knew he hated when I answered a question with a question. For your information, when I do that, I am gathering information to answer his original question. He should have known this after twelve years of marriage to me. "On my pants." He grit out in a reasonable and calm voice.

I picked up my wonder woman coffee mug and took a sip, then I responded in a similarly calm voice. "Then you are likely to find it in the dryer."

Less calmly, he rushed over to the laundry area. Slamming open the door, he boomed incredulously. Though he shouldn't have, this wasn't the first time this scene had played. "You washed my belt?"

I sorted my stack into a labeled manilla folder. "I washed your pants."

"Why didn't you take the belt off of the pants?" he hollered while frantically checking over the contents of the dryer, dumping the clean clothes one by one onto the unswept floor.

"Why didn't you?" I countered.

He found the pants. Sure enough, the belt was attached. Now it was squeaky clean. He sauntered over to me suggestively. "I wasn't exactly thinking of my belt when I took off my pants."

Ignoring his innuendo, I pushed away from the sorting table to begin packing my lunch for work. "Maybe you should have."

"Ah man," I didn't see him because my head was in the refrigerator, but I heard him slide his pants up his legs and groan. "You washed my wallet too." I considered apple or orange. "What is this, the third time?"

I decided to take them both. "I couldn't say."

"You should check pockets before running laundry."

He was now in my line of sight as I stuffed my lunch box. I sniffed haughtily. "I maintain that the owner of the pants in question should empty the pockets."

He plopped a crisply laundered wad of dollar bills onto the counter next to me. "The person who does the laundry should check pockets and pretreat for stains."

I blinked at him serenely while I scooped the dollars into my bathrobe. "Should we take a survey on this?"

Turning from me to grab his own cup of coffee, he mumbled. "No more studies. I will do the laundry from now on."

"You're only saying that because you would lose."

He sipped his coffee and glared at me. "I am only saying this because I don't want to purchase more than one new wallet in a year."

Lucy: You are an evil genius.

Candace: I think the launderer should check pockets. It is part of the process.

Miriam: Not the point, Candace.

Me: His pockets, his stuff. Besides, I have been encouraging him to do it sooner by taking a load over myself. He often takes it out of my hands before I can get all the way there.

And speaking of laundry, Miriam didn't let anyone else do her laundry. Ever. She had seen done all the wrong ways because Bob was a bachelor with five roommates a long time before she came along and she had a lot to correct. For instance: The **invisible barrier** over the laundry basket.

A twenty-year-old Miriam woke dreamily from yet another night not in her own bed. This was becoming a pattern, a gloriously luxurious pattern. She leaned over to stroke Bob's bulging deltoid muscle, trailing her fingers down into the brachial radials she'd been studying in her anatomy class. His anatomy was not that of the laboratory cadavers. He was warm and responsive and alive. And his name was Bob, of all things. She'd never imagined herself with someone named Bob. Bob sounded like an accountant, not this sexual beast.

She had to cut her study of her own personal muscle man short for her own natural urges. Coming back from the bathroom, she was still in a heady daze when she tripped over a pile of clothes on the floor. Clothes was a generous word, she was soon to discover, as the morning light revealed a mass of tangled, partially ripped body coverings. They lazily trailed Labyrinthine toward a clean, white wicker basket. So clean, in fact, that if this were a mickey mouse cartoon, it would twinkle.

Taking a swift breath of air through her mouth, she dove downward, scooped up the path and shoved it into the basket. Floor free of hazards, she crawled back beneath the sheets, marveling at what an awesome girl friend she was.

She woke lazily to an empty bed and the return of the mess on the floor. Worse, Bob seemed to be pawing through the ruined clothes frantically. She yawned loudly, alerting her boyfriend that she was awake. His pawing paused. She sat up in bed and glanced at his left hand, still holding a purple shirt he'd extricated from the mass. Bob followed her gaze. "I needed a clean shirt."

"Those aren't clean," Miriam said.

"They were before you stuffed them into my laundry basket."

"If your clean clothes are on your floor, what's in your closet?" she asked.

Bob crawled onto the bed sexily forming his body on top of hers, a move she'd already learned meant that he was about to say something she didn't approve of. "My winter wardrobe."

How the invisible barrier managed to cover the laundry basket in the first place was this: Bob didn't trust that clothes wouldn't mold. Post-shower towels and workout clothes were deemed too wet and needed to air dry before he would trust them inside the laundry basket. So he hung them over the empty laundry basket to dry, covering the receptacle from other deserving items.

The fix? According to Miriam, she puts the wet stuff directly into the washer. Which leads us to the next launderer type: **The wash and forget.**

Bob's roommate Shane only came out of his basement to start or change the washing machine. Miriam had been staying at Bob's place for weeks on end before discovering the existence of this person. Since staying at Bob's, she had taken to running a load of Bob's underwear with her own necessities. The man could wear the same T-shirt over and over again to classes but would have rather bought new underwear than wear yesterday's pair. It was one of the reasons she suspected she would be marrying him some day.

She had her perfectly sorted clothes in a basket she had purchased and stored in Bob's room. She carried it with her to the dingy, ill-used laundry room and opened the lid of the washer, fully expecting it to be empty because… dudes. This was not the case. The smell emanating from the gaping hole of the machine was enough to make a normal person gag. Miriam was made of sterner stuff than that. She did have four brothers after all, and she had been staying in this dive for weeks on end. She took a gulping breath of air and peered in to find a fully loaded a moldy pile of clothes. How long had this been in there? She wondered. She shut the lid with her elbow and set down her basket.

She then went knocking on the other roommates' doors to let them know they would have to rerun. The other two had no knowledge of the laundry in the washer. Probably because they hadn't done laundry in a very long time, as evidenced by their own yellow brick roads of laundry. Bob was perched on the edge of the couch typing a term paper on a desktop computer when she asked him about the clothes, fairly certain that it would be the end of their relationship if they were his.

"Must be Shane's," he said without glancing away from the glowing green screen.

"Who is Shane?"

"Lives under the stairs. Pays rent by envelope."

"There's a room under the stairs?"

"I wouldn't call it a room."

"Bob, I need to do laundry." She sighed one of those completely beleaguered female sighs. Bob snapped his head around in new relationship alertness. "I think I might as well go to my mother's," she said wearily.

Some instinct must have told Bob not to let this girl walk out of his life. He stood from his desk without saving the document to a floppy disk and followed her into the laundry nook. Opening the lid, Bob reeled backward. He tripped over Miriam in his haste to make it to a sink, where he unleashed the contents of a breakfast that was partially digested in his stomach. That done, he gurgled some water and looked for a towel to cover his nose with. Miriam watched him curiously and, luckily for Bob, not with much disgust. In a show most manly, Bob reached his bare hands into the machine, dug out the moldering wet piece of fabric, and heaved them all the way to the stairs where he let them fall with a satisfyingly squishy plop. The smell immediately began to permeate the room, and Bob had to make another hasty retreat to the bathroom sink. Bob's always had a sensitive gag reflex.

The smell was soon so potent that the door under the stairs opened. A frizzy red haired head emerged to find short stern Miriam in wait. "Your laundry probably needs to be redone."

The young man who must have been Shane blinked at her twice. "How long have you lived here?" he asked in a rusty, unused voice. Then he glanced at the pile of disgusting clothes. On top was a Grateful Dead tie-dyed shirt. Shane visibly brightened, picked it up, then wrinkled his nose in distaste. "What time is it?"

"4 o'clock Sunday."

"Sunday? Really? Already?"

And Miriam really couldn't help herself from asking. "What day did you think it was?"

"Friday. I put these in on Friday for a job interview on Monday."

Miriam nodded, as if that made perfect sense. And it did. Why else would anyone in this house actually start a load of laundry?

He swept the clothes into his cavelike room, somehow understanding that the washer would not be free right now for him to re run the clothes. Then glancing at Miriam, he said in a not so rusty voice, "Hey nice to meet you."

"Miriam," she answered.

"Miriam," he smiled. That was probably the first and last time she met Shane, who moved out shortly after that for a job in LA.

According to Miriam, the wash and forget has been corrected by doing laundry Every. Single. Day. But then a person has to do laundry Every. Single. Day. I am not sure this is the perfect fix.

While she was probably too understanding of Shane's foible. This next one was just laughable: **Mixing the wrong colors.**

Bob's upstairs roommate, Mario, wore pink underwear, which Miriam first found out the night Bob taught her to play beer pong. Miriam had been a sheltered good girl until meeting Bob, who made it his new life's purpose to not only keep this amazing girl, but to show her an amazing time. Bob exposed her to the wonders of the chilli dog and now beer pong. Miriam was terrible at it, which meant she was really drunk very early in the evening.

Having reached capacity, Miriam stumbled up the stairs to the bathroom outside of Bob's room. Being drunk, she didn't particularly pay attention to noises like singing or water running. She slammed open the bathroom door so that it banged a dent in the wall. It wasn't the first dent in this particular wall and wouldn't be the last. Hovering over the toilet seat, because she was not sure the toilet had ever been scrubbed, Miriam let loose with a sigh of relief. That taken care of, she stumblingly pulled up her tight jeans. In bending over, she found a pair of pink tighty whities. Funny, she'd never seen a pink version before.

At that moment, she realized she was not alone. She realized this because the white noise of a shower running had most abruptly shut off. Swiveling her head toward the silent shower, Miriam found herself caught in the act: holding up and examining a man's pink underwear in front of the man himself.

Mario winked at her from behind the thankfully black shower curtain. "I don't think they'll fit you."

With a squeak, Miriam dropped the underwear she had no idea she'd even picked up and ducked out of the bathroom. The guys laughed about it later and she and Mario developed a friendship despite the pink underwear that remained a curiosity. More so when they all learned that if given enough encouragement at parties, Mario also had the tendency to streak. Something would trigger him. Either a dare, or finally reaching that capacity for drunkenness one needs for college shenanigans to ensue. He streaked at beach parties, at Christmas parties, at the homecoming football game in their senior year, at Miriam's graduation party. Always leaving behind pink underwear. She'd never seen another color, and he didn't ever wear pink outside of his underwear. Then again, the man wore the same red sweater and black t-shirt and pants the entire time that she knew him.

Finally, the night of her graduation party, she and Bob had decided that graduation meant getting their own place together. Miriam gathered up the courage and asked Mario about the pink underwear. "Is your favorite color pink?" she asked after gathering his clothes up and handing them over.

Mario may have loved to streak, but his exit strategy and return to normal was never really well planned out. He gave her a confused look. "Why would you say that?"

Which in Miriam's book was not really an answer. "You always wear pink underwear."

The side of Mario's mouth cocked up in a flirtatious half grin. "You checking out my drawers?"

She glanced disdainfully down at his still nude form. "How could I not?"

"I always liked you," he grinned.

She shifted on her feet uncomfortably. "Would you just make us all more comfortable and put on your pink tighty whities?"

Obligingly, he began to pull on his clothes. First the underwear, next the black shirt and pants, followed by the red sweater. "You really wanna know?"

"I wouldn't have asked if I wasn't curious."

"My Ma sends me clothes. And I have sensitive skin, so I have to wash them before I wear them."

She cocked her head to the side, trying to decide if this was an answer.

Mario rolled his eyes. "The underwear are white when they arrive. After I wash them, they come out pink."

Miriam goggled. "How?"

Mario shrugged. "You tell me. It's the same thing every couple of months, black pants, red sweater, underwear."

She should have known. She didn't, but the evidence had been there the whole time.

According to Miriam, the pink underwear usually is the fix for the problem of mixing the wrong colors. Mario just had never had anyone explain it to him before. So she did.

The real reason Bob and Miriam are married today, I think, is because of Sam. Sam liked to help every so often, when he was between terms of medical laboratory science school. He would come through the house like a whirlwind of activity. Scooping up garbage, dusting lampshades, and washing and folding all manner of laundry including sheets, towels and in one very significant incident, Miriam's only interview shirt right before her own Medical School interviews.

The men of the house had grown complacent with a woman in their midst. Bob and Miriam had been inseparable for a year and a half. She smelled nice. She filled the refrigerator and hung new towels in the bathrooms. Sam, thinking to return the favor, scooped up a pile of Bob's clothes and Miriam's laundry basket. He dumped all items in the washer, set a timer, and even returned to switch the load to the dryer. What the poor young man failed to realize is that not all female clothes are the same. For instance, when silk is dried on high with a load of towels, it turns into the texture of terrycloth.

On the day of her medical school interview, Miriam flew out of Bob's room in a rage fifteen minutes before her scheduled time, hefting an empty laundry basket like a weapon, clad only in a purple see through bra. "Where is it?" she demanded.

Instead of ogling her, as most college boys would have, these brave men cowered behind Bob, who bravely stood in front of the knife block in the kitchen. Her bosom heaving like a romance novel heroine, Miriam grabbed Bob by the ear, pulling him down to her level. "Where is it?" she said, her hot breath singing his eye balls.

Bob began to shake like a leaf. "I don't know what you want."

She let go of his ear to peer menacingly around his shoulder. Bob cowered and melted away, allowing her wrath to fall on the two other men present. Mario blinked uncomprehendingly at her, but wisely kept his mouth shut. Sam tucked his hand behind his back and skirted out of the kitchen. He tucked himself behind the wall, then answered. "I started a load of laundry for you. Are you looking for something in particular?"

"Like a shirt." Mario coughed.

Miriam glared daggers at him. Then hefted a knife from the block Bob had unwittingly left unguarded. The knife stuck in the wall that protected Sam, quivering with the rage she had yet to unleash on the three boys. Through clenched teeth, Miriam said, "I have an interview in fifteen minutes. It is the most important interview of my life. If you value your lives, you better hope I have something to wear to that interview." Then she stormed down into the basement laundry room to find a shirt that was most likely in ruins.

Without a thought, all men left the house until the storm passed, leaving the knife embedded in the wall. Brave Bob used his time to race over to the nearest clothing store, a Sax Fifth Avenue, normally an eight-minute drive away. Upon entry to this ritzy store, Bob was assailed by a suspicious clerk. He blurted out what he needed and the damage that had been done. The woman took pity on him, plucked a shirt that cost his entire month's pay from the racks and rang it up. He was back in under ten minutes.

He bent down on one knee, presenting her with the shirt, eyes shut tight, cringingly.

Seeing the price tag on this replacement, Miriam was so blown away by the gesture and the self sacrificing apology that she said "Yes."

Bob really didn't know he'd even asked her a question until wedding plans were underway.

After having spent a year and a half with these disgusting men, Miriam had decided that Bob was by far the most trainable of the lot.

Sam told that story at their wedding and Miriam gave him the stink-eye, which caused him to duck under the nearest table.

So in essence, Bob ended an argument about laundry with a marriage proposal. Somehow I don't see that working out every time.

***

A week into what Lucy had named The Dish War, all capitals, Candace found herself yelling at Joey for rinsing a fork in the sink. "Do not help your father."

"I am not helping him," her thirteen-year-old son whined. "I am cleaning a fork for me." He shifted a pile of crusty plates from the sink to the crumb covered counter top so he could reach the faucet.

She watched sternly, making sure that was all he did. "We will not give quarter to the enemy," she grumbled, sniffing importantly.

Joey didn't smile at her General Patton impression. He shut off the water, dried the fork with his shirt and picked up the top plate from the pile. He inspected it for crusted sauces. Finding only crumbs, he shook it over the sink, tucked it under his arm and saluted his mom. "I am protecting my loved ones from becoming casualties of war." Then he left. Candace was left with the feeling of not knowing whether she should laugh or cry.

Candace ended the Dishwar the next day. She began by throwing out every dirty dish in the sink. By this time, the layer of food had crystalized into some impenetrable substance that probably should have been studied by the military. I asked for a sample, but she couldn't chip a piece off. Harriet took great pleasure in this endeavor by ruthlessly smashing the plates into the garbage can and listening to the loud noises made. Karin hid in her room with her headphones on.

Next, leaving Joey in charge of the girls, she took herself to the most exclusive kitchen store in the area and bought every pot, pan, plate, and cup that she had ever drooled over in a home magazine. She had them delivered to the house because it was too much to fit in the car. Upon their arrival the following day, she carefully unpacked each item. She breathed in the fresh sent of packing peanuts contentedly. She finished by cooking a gourmet meal for herself, ordering pizza for the kids. The leftovers were packaged away in brand new Tupperware before Paul came home from a twelve-hour shift. He never asked about it.

Lesson learned: There is something to be gained from every argument. Also, never touch Miriam's silk blouses.

Chapter 7

Unpack and Redistribute the Mental Load

Lucy: It's summer camp signup time.

Me: It's February.

Candace: She's almost late for some of the cutoffs.

Me: It's February.

Lucy: I just hate having to remember to do this and the doctor's visits, and to shop for new school clothes and school supplies.

Candace: And the finances and the house maintenance schedule, the vacation.

Miriam: Setting up playdates and remembering their friend's mom's names. *Looking at us, her kid's friend's moms* What? I have baby-brain.

Me: How come they aren't doing any of this?

Candace: Paul could. He would do it poorly, but he could.

Miriam: If I make Bob a list....

Lucy: He can have mine. I make lists of everything and I still forget.

Me: How did this become our job?

Candace: Well you see Jenna, when Paul goes to work, he thinks about work.

Me: When I am at work, the schools do always call me, not Clifford.

Lucy: Society made us this way.

Candace: Maternity leave made us this way. I just never stopped.

Me: We have to do something.

Lucy: Uh oh. Another Jenna assignment.

Miriam: Bob helps. At least right now. Please don't make this worse, Jenna.

Me: Haven't I been helping?

We all look at Miriam's bulging belly, sighing.

Candace: Let's hear it.

Me: We take off for the week with no notice to the family. The guys have to cover it all.

Candace: Ok, I like this plan.

Lucy: Sign me up.

Miriam: But when we come back...

Candace: So much cleaning.

Lucy: So much appreciation.

Me: That's just it. We do as little as possible when we come back.

Miriam: This is not a good plan.

Me: How else can you think to reset? Also, we shouldn't bring our phones.

Candace: No deal.

Lucy: Where are we going?

Miriam: I'd like to go back to what happens when we come back.

Me: When we come back, we will be given a report from our spouse of all the things that went horribly wrong. Then we sit down and divide up, fixing those things as a team.

Candace: Paul will never go for this.

Miriam: I should call my mother.

Lucy: It will be great.

This I do not tell them about. The weekend before we leave, my house.

Clifford cleared the dishwasher while I sat at our counter, glasses perched on my nose, running through my latest set of statistics. "They agreed to the weekend away?" He asked.

I crossed out a figure. "Yes. Please support the guys while we are gone. I don't know how many of them know we are leaving."

He snorted but continued about the business of drying a wine glass with a hand towel. "That will be interesting to watch."

I looked up from my work to roam my eyes down his casually muscular frame. "Not all husbands are as well equipped to run a household as you."

He rolled his eyes. "I had to learn quickly."

"Sorry." I mumbled, meaning it.

He leaned toward me across the counter and lifted the lenses from my face. "They still don't know."

I narrowed my now blurry eyes at him. "No, they still don't know."

"Jenna, they are not subjects in some science experiment. These are your best friends of ten years."

I snatched by glasses out of his hand. "I am trying to help them." Telling them wouldn't help them.

He ran a hand delicately along my cheek. "They need to know."

"Not yet."

He kissed my forehead. "If you don't, I will."

I sighed. "Can you just support me?"

He unbalanced me from my stool and wove his arms over me. Resting his chin on my head, he said, "I can do better than that."

***

Our girls weekend turned into a week. Things happened that should never be discussed in polite society. Let's just say that Lucy needed to clear her head. Miriam laughed so hard that she puked. Candace ignored all of

Paul's texts. And I had a marvelous time with my best friends.

***

Candace came home to a clean house. It was mid-afternoon, shortly after Joey was scheduled to be home from school. Right before the afternoon rush to the after-school activities began in earnest. She had timed her arrival, anticipating swooping in to offer unexpected assistance in the midst of the chaos. As a working, practically single mother all of these years, she had wished so many afternoons for some magical carpool fairy to come and rescue her. She felt that this was the perfect way to show her family how much she loved them.

She would be like the hero in the book she'd just finished while lounging by the pool at the overpriced resort I'd booked for us. Paul would be the harried heroine, overburdened by the duties of homework, lunches, laundry, and, of course, crying children. Candace would smile knowingly and say in a cowboy drawl, "Don't worry your pretty head, little lady. I've got this."

When she walked in, the fantasy shrank like a week-old birthday balloon. There was no chaos. There was no half folded pile of laundry adorning the armrests of the couch. There was no pile of open lunch boxes or even discarded take out boxes littering the counters. The floor did not feel sticky or crunchy in the slightest. Paul was not tearing out his hair as Harriet clutched to his pants leg, weeping that Karin refused yet again to play dolls with her. Paul was not even present in the downstairs hallway. Candace was starting to feel edgy. Perhaps she should have accepted some of his calls.

They must be home somewhere. Afterall, Joey was sitting alone at the kitchen table, with a book propped up in front of him. He nodded at her entry as if his mother returned from a weeklong sabbatical every other week. He even returned to his book without a hug or hello of any kind. It would have been the silent treatment except that he was a thirteen-year-old boy.

She heaved her flowered, hard plastic suitcase up the stairs on her own to deposit it onto her bedroom floor. She was impressed the zippers held. Curiously, there was no pile of laundry vomiting its overflow on to the floor. Paul did not suffer from an invisible laundry basket barrier like some other husbands we'd discussed. The bed was actually made, although her decorative pillows were nowhere to be found. Had he even slept here?

Instead of unpacking, Candace took a moment to explore these mysterious circumstances. She opened a linen closet, half expecting a maid to pop out. The door to Karin's room was propped open with an eye-patched teddy bear. The floor of her room, which hadn't seen daylight in at least three months, was now so sparkly she could imagine picnicking on it. The room was empty of human occupants.

She traveled further down the hall until she came upon Harriet's little used room. Here, she heard voices.

"One more pony slide, and then we get our shoes on for our city tour." That was Paul's voice, but confusingly, he sounded warm, calm and unstressed.

She creaked the door open. "Mommy!" Harriet dropped the pony she was holding and leapt into Candace's arms, nearly toppling her to the floor. Now this was the greeting she had missed from her surly teenager downstairs. Candace returned the exuberant embrace, inhaling the comfort of her daughter's hair.

She eyed Paul over the head of her little one. Paul's shirt was untucked. He wore stockings on his feet and his pants were cuffed at the ankles stylishly. He reminded her of the cool guy he'd been once upon a time. The cool guy who had swept her off her feet, who smoked cheroot, read poetry in coffee houses and believed in a less materialistic life. Now Candace understood what was going on. Her husband had been body snatched.

He was making his own perusal of her, running his eyes over her body possessively.

Little arms embraced her from behind. She clutched at her second girl automatically. "Who'd you hire to clean up the place?" the snarky words tumbled out of Candace's mouth and there was no shovel to put them back. She regretted them immediately, but couldn't seem to break eye contact until he offered an answer.

Paul lowered his eyes first, in order to nudge Harriet to the door. "Go get your shoes on."

When Paul returned his gaze to hers, she realized she'd been taken in by his lowered gaze. She'd thought she'd won some unspoken argument. The banked fire in his gaze was not desperation or lust, but teetering closer to rage. She knew she'd misspoken but couldn't back down and admit it or she'd lose the upper hand entirely. "Our kids can be very helpful if properly motivated," he said softly.

This time, Candace pulled away and nudged Karin. "Do as your father says," Karin slipped out of the room as silently as she'd come in. Candace looked around the room. "Where's Harriet? I thought you told her to put her shoes on."

"I did, and she is," he nodded importantly.

Candace rested her hands on her hips. "How do you know she is?" In Candace's experience, it took Harriet no less than three reminders to actually do what she was told.

"Because I trust her," Paul said simply.

Well, Candace did not. She had experience to back her up. She left the room in search of Harriet, certain that she would find her barefoot and wrestling with a stuffed dinosaur, or breaking out the glitter. Instead, the sight that rooted Candace to the bottom step was Harriet. She was tying the laces of a new pair of sketchers, her little tongue jammed into the corner of her mouth in concentration. "You need help there?" Candace offered, past the lump in her throat.

Harriet stood up and wiggled a shoe adorned by a loosely but perfectly tied shoelace. "Look what Daddy taught me."

Candace felt like she'd been slapped. Her head was spinning so much that when she actually turned around on the stair, she nearly toppled into Paul. The smug bastard rested his hands supportively on the outsides of Candace's shoulders. "She can tie her shoes," Candace said.

"Yes, she can." It would have been a perfectly magical moment if Paul, this one time, had not kept talking. "You see Candace, children just want to learn and do new things."

Karin had the beautiful timing to hop down the stairs at that moment, attempting to bypass her parent's altercation. Candace grabbed her arm and lifted her sleeve, checking frantically for marks. "Did you beat them?"

Karin tugged her arm. "Ow. Mom, give me my arm back." She gave her mother a look that clearly questioned her sanity.

Meanwhile, smug Paul kept on talking in a soothing medical practitioner's voice that he knew grated Candace's nerves. "No, Candace, of course not. Why would you think that?"

Her stomach dipped like the bottom of a rollercoaster. Candace felt that she must be in an episode of the Twilight Zone. "Then how?"

"They just needed to be shown how to do things, and given the opportunity to shine." He leaned against the wall, crossing his arms over his chest. "It is not unlike training a resident at the hospital."

"I wouldn't know," Candace grumbled, tucking her arms underneath her breasts glancing around the clearly maintained household. A household she'd been fighting tooth and nail to maintain since Joey took his first breath. A household that had both suffocated and upheld her self-worth. She felt keenly the snuggles, the exhaustion, the helplessness of the years. Obviously, all of that struggle was nothing to this man. "How did you get the time off? You never take time off."

"I shuffled a few things in my day so I wouldn't have to work at night." He turned to Karin then helping her to remove herself from her mother. "Get your coat." Then right back to Candace, he said, "I can always chart from home." He reached up to embrace her.

She shrugged him off, building rage choking her throat. "You never have before." She stormed the rest of the way down the stairs, gesturing wildly to encompass the three children, the large clean great room and kitchen. "I have been doing all of this alone. For years." That last part cringingly ended in a wail.

Joey glanced up from his book, then sunk lower in his chair. The girls both stopped what they were doing to watch the show. Paul observed her cautiously stepping toward the kitchen counter. With a single head tilt, he broke the frozen spell on the girls who shuffled to the car. Both parents watched the door click shut behind them.

"You make it too hard on yourself, you know," Paul said, drawing her attention back to him with laser precision. "You enabled these kids to walk all over you."

Candace's jaw fell open. This time she couldn't form words on top of the rage overtaking her. She felt her cheeks warm. Clearly not wishing to witness the brutal murder of his father, Joey slammed his book shut, tucked it under an arm, and fled upstairs.

Candace shut her eyes. The sight of Paul, her husband of fifteen years, made her want to puke, preferably, on him. "How dare you."

Paul was obviously oblivious to the danger he was in because he continued speaking. "How dare I?"

"You have been with them a week and you dare to make judgements about how I raise them?" Her voice was raising in volume and her feet itched to pace. Candace held herself still, afraid she might physically attack this person she shared a house with. "Where were you when I was doing this alone for the past thirteen years?"

Paul blinked rapidly while Candace clutched the cold counter slab island in front of her with white knuckles. "There are three of them. You hardly made them alone."

"Shut the fuck up." Had she thought before speaking, she probably would not have resorted to swearing at him, giving him ammo to question her sanity, but desperate times. "Before they could fend for themselves. When there were noses to be wiped and clothes to be washed and lessons to be taught." She slapped her hand against the counter to punctuate each task on the list.

"I bathed them, fed them, read to them, checked their homework. Where were you?"

Paul smartly maintained a safe distance away by choosing this opportunity to don a coat from the closet near the front doorway. "I know it was hard while I was in medical school, Candy, but that was a dozen years ago."

She grabbed a banana out of the fruit bowl in front of her and pointed it at the stairs toward Harriet's room. "If it was a dozen years ago, what were you doing last year when I had a child home with me all day long and still had to fit in my work?"

She waited, but he didn't have a snarky comment to offer her, just a snarky raised eyebrow. She went on before he could open his fat mouth again. "This was the first year that I didn't have to share a bed with a kicking child. I still have to drive them to kingdom come, plan their meals, their extra-curricular activities, go to the parent-teacher conferences, clean this house. If you could chart from home, why haven't you been helping me?"

While she took a breath, he got his word in. "You underestimate our children."

"I what now?"

"Oh, you heard me." He placed a knowing paternal hand on his hip. "Kids in Uganda prep meals for their family at three."

"Good for them."

"I am just saying this parenting thing isn't as hard as you make it." He glanced down at his watch.

"I am expected to be perfect every day. The perfect career woman. The perfect wife. Amiable, competent, clean. Like Mary-Fucking-Poppins."

"Who expects you to be?"

She didn't acknowledge his speaking and gave into rage pacing. "You have them for a week and you have it all figured out."

He stepped forward as if he would reach for her, but thought better of it. "I am just saying that you don't have to hold yourself to those standards. They can help. They can learn if you let them."

"I don't have these standards. I don't give a shit about standards. But the law says I could be arrested if I don't accompany my child to the park or if I let them play with knives. If something goes wrong."

"Well, it's real nice that you have come back from a week long vacation to God knows where, energized to fight the fight for womanhood everywhere, but some of us have to get the kids to their activities." He gripped the doorknob and then shot a parting line over his shoulder. "So why don't you unpack your bags, have a bubble bath and calm the fuck down."

If Candace's head could have exploded with rage, it would have. But Paul wasn't around to witness the carnage.

***

"So if I am understanding this correctly, we are mad at my brother for cleaning the kitchen and bedroom and teaching Harriet to tie her shoes?" Lucy asked while sweeping a stack of unsorted mail from the table. She replaced the garbage mail with a steaming bowl of Miriam soup reheated for just such an emergency. "The bastard."

Candace rested her arms on the table, then slumped her whole head onto them. A piece of hair drifted into the soup. "It's not that. It's the first fifteen years of marriage before that."

Lucy propped her feet up on a stack of folded towels on the chair between them. Candace marveled that Lucy had made such an impressive dent in the carnage she had come home to. "The man did better than we expected when we left. Should he really be blamed for that?"

Candace eyeballed her friend. "Are you really not seeing this? Or are you messing with me?"

Lucy patted her foot. "Why don't you explain it to me again?"

Candace groaned.

Miriam shuffled over and placed a second bowl in front of Lucy. "Stop being dense. We are mad at him because he could have been helping all along and hasn't."

"But maybe he will now," Lucy tried.

Miriam took her own seat at the table and said quietly. "It might be too late."

Lucy grimaced. "So, how long are you staying?"

"You have to see this through Candace," Miriam said. "You have to go home and give him a chance."

She wouldn't have listened to Lucy, who had to love Paul. He was, after all, her flesh and blood. But Miriam had no reason to love Paul.

So she went home.

Paul showed up on Lucy's doorstep with a hastily packed bag and a boatload of confusion the very next night.

***

Miriam had arrived home to an exhausted Bob, a cranky mother, a puking child and some mysterious stain on the ceiling over her toilet.

Bob hugged her, whispering frantically, "Please don't ever leave me with her again." He was, of course, referring to Miriam's mother, who had an even worse temper than pregnant Miriam. The displeasure radiating off of her mother was made all the more intense by the fact that she only spoke fluent Spanish faster than Bob's high school Spanish could interpret.

Miriam had been in constant contact with both her mother and Bob while we were gone. She'd read some of their text messages to us. Some nights we scrolled through them while munching on popcorn while Miriam read them with inflections that seemed in line with a Shakespearean comedy.

After escorting her mother to the door and refilling John's humidifier, Miriam found herself slumped on their well-worn couch next to Bob. Bob already had a beer in hand. He'd forgotten to fix anything for dinner for Miriam. She watched him contentedly as he surfed the tv for a Telenovela. She had missed this quiet. This comfort of not having to speak, but just to be with another person. She had missed him.

After a time, she hoisted her bulk from the couch to fix herself a plate of whatever her mother had left in the refrigerator. Shutting the door, she jumped back, startled at the sudden appearance of her husband. "Did you have a nice adventure?"

"I think we all did," she said through the half tamale she'd stuffed in her face.

"Was it really necessary to have that woman here to watch me?"

Miriam cocked her head to the side. "Watch you? She was here to help."

Bob put his hands in his pockets in that nonthreatening passive aggressive stance he sometimes took with her. She'd noticed he'd been doing this a lot since the pregnancy. "She criticized everything I did. It was like living with a school yard nun."

Miriam swallowed another bite, leaning against the yellowed counter behind the refrigerator. "How could you tell? You can't exactly understand her."

"Oh, I could tell."

Miriam bit the inside of her cheek, trying not to laugh at some of the things she remembered from her mother's texts. Bob did seem broken up about this. She leaned toward him, attempting to brush his waistband with her ripe pregnant breasts. She knew he'd missed her. Maybe she could make it up to him. However, he stepped back, still semi glaring. Miriam pouted.

"Why did you have her here?"

"To help you."

"I took the days off. You knew that. You don't need the help. Why should I?"

Miriam scoffed. "Because."

He raised an eyebrow. "Because..." he trailed off expectantly.

She didn't know what he wanted her to say. That he was a terrible cook and might end up poisoning their son. That he often got caught up in silly projects and could easily forget about their son. "I am just scared, you know?"

"Of what?" This time, his voice softened, and he allowed her to fold into his arms. "There's only one of him and one of me."

"Not for long," she mumbled into his shirt. How she hated these pregnancy hormones, she could already feel the needle prick of tears. "We don't know how to take care of two."

"Lots of people do it. Lots of men do it."

"Not my father," Miriam said, surprising herself. She hadn't thought about her father, or rather lack of father, in a long time. Her mother had never seemed to need him or miss him. He'd stayed long enough for a second child to be born and then drifted off to god knew where, never to be spoken of or thought of again.

Bob's arms tightened around her. "I have some bad news for you, if you think that's how it goes with men." He shifted her back so she could look at him. "You're never getting rid of me."

Then the tears fell in earnest. They were just getting to the good part when the phone rang. It was Lucy, requesting soup and comfort.

Me: So success?

Lucy: I got a lot of gratitude from Jonas. And now he's being super clingy.

Miriam: I guess Bob was always helpful. I just didn't trust him.

Me: Interesting. *Writing*

Lucy: What are you writing?

Me: Notes to myself about some research I am doing, so I don't forget.

Lucy: Why do you always end up writing when we are talking?

Me: I am always writing. Not just when I am with you.

Miriam: Good, because Candace would be pissed if she thought you were writing about us.

Lucy: Don't say her name, she might appear.

Me: Which one is staying with you now?

Lucy: Him.

Miriam: That should be fine. You've lived together before.

Lucy: When we were kids, and I thought I would be rid of him by now.

Miriam: Family is important. I hope these little ones will have a relationship like you two as adults.

Lucy: Luke warm? Barely tolerating each other?

Me: You like each other's spouses and live in the same city.

Lucy: If Paul stays at my house much longer, I am planning on moving.

Lesson Learned: Men aren't as helpless as they let us believe. And are highly offended when we suggest they are helpless at all.

Chapter 8

If You Want Something Done Right, Ask for Help.

Lucy: Here's your invitations bitches!

Me: Kegger?

Miriam *reading*: Better. A kid's birthday party.

Lucy: You are my daughter's aunties. I fully expect you all there.

Me: Awe chosen relatives are way better than awkward blood relations

Lucy: Speaking of awkward blood relations, Candace, please take mine back, just for the party.

Candace: What do I get out of this?

Lucy: The joy of not ruining two seven-year-olds' birthday party with their mother retiring to the nuthouse.

Me: That bad?

Candace: Because I love you, I will.

Lucy: Thank god my mother isn't flying in.

Miriam: What's wrong with your mother?

Candace: That woman always finds a way to pull all the drama onto herself.

Lucy: And she's a terrible gift giver.

Miriam: Doesn't she want to see her granddaughters?

Lucy: She and Danielle had a falling out. Something about being too similar.

Me: That should probably be part of the dating process before genetic co-mingling.

Candace: That would dramatically reduce the birth rate. I think everyone has a crazy relative.

Me: You're really taking him back then?

Candace: My shrink says I should.

Lucy: Thank god. I have enough problems with Jonas around. I don't need my brother there too.

Me: Maybe you can get him to help with the party.

Lucy: My brother?

Me: Jonas.

Lucy: Yeah right, when has a husband ever helped with a kids' party?

Me: You could delegate a task for him to be in charge of to start.

Candace: She'd have to choose something she can afford to go wrong.

Miriam: Like the presents?

Lucy: If I must.

Me: A delegated task gives him a sense of purpose and makes him feel more involved in the whole process.

Lucy stumbled down the stairs early Sunday morning and slumped on to the couch beside Danielle. The dog hopped up onto her lap to rest his bushy head on her shoulder. The better to reach her ear with his sopping wet tongue. Lucy could barely blink as she was still in her melatonin haze. Jonas, familiar with the routine, took her hand and placed a steaming cup of something caffeinated into her grip. She spilled a little on the dog's snout. The dog whimpered and flopped off of her lap onto the floor. Once free of this weight, Lucy tucked her feet beneath Danielle's bottom and blinked her eyes all the way open.

Seeing the new alertness of his wife's demeanor, Jonas judged the moment appropriate to speak. Twelve years of marriage had taught him well. "What is on the agenda for today, sergeant?" He'd developed the pet name for Lucy after the insane cleaning regimen she put them through every weekend since the purchase of their house two years ago.

Much negotiation of terms had ensued to get Lucy and Jonas to this happy place. Now his only act of defiance remaining in the face of sergeant Lucy was a pet name. One would think that all of the yoga she did during the week would chill her out on house duties. One would be wrong.

She blinked at him incredulously. "The girls' birthday is today at 2."

He took a bite of a sesame scone. "I thought that was next weekend."

Lucy took a moment to yoga breath, in through her nose, out through her mouth. She had only discussed this event with him to the miniscule detail three times a day for the last two weeks. She checked for a gleam in the eye that meant he was kidding. He was not. She was going to kill Jenna for suggesting she give him any responsibility for this party.

Their daughter, unaware of the tension between her parents, decided to share her joy. "Oh, it is today," Danielle said in her excited voice. "Mommy ordered a bounce house."

"Great. Everything is ready then," Jonas said.

Danielle shook her head sadly. "Oh Daddy. Stop talking."

When she recovered from her minor stroke, Lucy said, "Jonas, you are to keep the girls out of the house until 130."

He looked at the clock on the stove, which blinked an unhelpful 7:43. "Starting when?"

"Starting with the softball game, they are in at 10," Lucy said.

"We bring snack this week," Danielle chirped help-fully.

Jonas' eyes bugged. "What are we bringing for snack?"

Lucy sipped the last dregs of her drink, then cupped the empty mug within her hands to absorb the remaining heat. "I don't know, but I am sure you will figure it out."

"Emily is still sleeping. Are you sure it is at 10?" Jonas asked, a slight note of panic creeping into his voice.

"I am sure. You'd better wake her." Lucy got up from the couch, carrying her mug and the plates from Danielle's breakfast to the sink. "Thanks for letting me sleep in by the way."

Jonas got up as well, fearfully anticipating waking Emily. Emily woke up like her mother, but wasn't old enough for coffee yet. "I can't tell if you're being sarcastic or not."

Lucy turned on the faucet. "Neither can I."

***

We pulled up to their house promptly at 2pm because Clifford has a thing about being late to places. As Clifford slowed at the curb, we were almost T-boned by a white minivan pulling into their driveway. I watched from the safety of my seat belt as Jonas slammed open the automatic doors, hustling the girls out of the car. Emily's side ponytail drooped in the classic Dad hair style.

Danielle ran up to our car to unload my children. "I slid home," she chirped, showing the big dusty swipe down her white uniform leg.

"Danielle," Jonas hissed. "You have to get dressed for your party." Emily had already entered the house, leaving their front door wide open. The dog scooched Danielle to the side so that he could reach his giant head into Steven's car seat. "You know you take forever to get ready," Jonas hollered as he pried the dog from my giggling, still buckled son.

Becca was out of the car in a flash. She grabbed Danielle's hand and the two girls shrieked into the house. Steven stayed helplessly buckled while the dog feasted on loose cheerios in ticklish spots, completely disregarding the frantic tugging of his collar.

I decided that now was as good a time as any to help. I unstrapped myself, then leaned between the two front seats to unstrap Steven, wiping his face with my sleeve. Clifford went out of his side to get the gifts. The dog, now unloaded, Jonas, left us to hustle into his house. Clifford hefted his newsprint wrapped bulk. "What did we get them again?"

"Power tools."

"Jenna." It is truly amazing how much feeling one word can convey when uttered by my husband.

"I included a gift receipt in case they want to return them."

"Are power tools really appropriate for little girls?" He puffed, nearly tripping over the stoop. I marveled that he knew I wasn't being sarcastic.

"Don't be so gendered," I said, swaying Steven's hand in mine as we crossed over the threshold.

He unloaded the gift onto the first table he could find, then flexed his fingers to return blood flow. "If you think I believe this is a fit present for a seven-year-old boy or girl, you don't know me at all."

"You've met them."

"Fair point." With that, he wandered off to find a beer.

I found Lucy with her head inside of the fridge while simultaneously clutching a mimosa. "Are we the first to arrive?" I asked.

"Thank god," she sighed.

My son, having abandoned me for the dog, left me with a hand free to steal her drink. I took a sip, then winced at the burn. She left it to me so that she could gallop up the stairs to check on Danielle's progress. From downstairs I could hear the little girl shriek, "No Mom, you can't touch my hair," followed by a door slam and an inhuman howl.

I decided to check out the kitchen for some way to help with food. From the other side of the bar, I caught the dog with his paws up on the counter sniffing at the saran-wrapped appetizers Lucy must have found on Pinterest. I looped around the bar to grab his collar. Only a well-placed knee to the chest levered him down. I dragged him to the garage and slammed the door in his sad doggy face. Task complete, I glanced out the windows into the backyard. They got lucky with the appearance of sun in late February. The bounce house was up and my children were already in it. Short patio tables had been set up in the back with pink and green plastic covers tied around the legs. Balloon centerpieces floated drowsily from bowls filled with water and fake frogs and Lilly pads. She'd even thought to set up a shoe bin at the edge of the grass for parents to locate their children's lost shoes while said children bounced unaware.

When she came back downstairs, Lucy nudged me with her hip to get my attention. I handed her drink back. She downed the glass in a single gulp, then offered me one she'd pulled from somewhere unknown. "Looks great," I said, meaning it. "What's the theme?"

"Princess frog ninja."

I nodded like this was a common birthday party theme. "Where does the ninja come in?"

"Epic battle later, after we have all drunk enough punch."

"What did you decide was Jonas' job?"

"Dog duty."

Miriam and Bob let themselves in without ringing the doorbell. Bob carried John like a monkey on his back while Miriam daintily deposited two bagged presents. Bob escorted Miriam over to us, his hand trailing along his wife's plump backside. "I'll keep the monkey if you drive home later." He kissed her cheek without receiving a response, then headed off for the tv and presumably Jonas' scotch stash.

"John's been clinging to Bob all week," she explained while inspecting the food beneath the wrappings. "We think he figured out there was another baby on the way."

"At least he isn't clinging to you," I said. "The kid looks like he enjoys his tamales."

Lucy began to explain the different appetizers to Miriam when Candace and Paul arrived. We weren't sure if they were going to arrive together or not, as Paul had officially moved back last weekend. Candace had co-erced Paul into going to counseling with her.

"They are your nieces, Paul," Candace chastised as they marched their way into the house. "You have to make an appearance." Looked like counseling hadn't changed all that much yet.

"But Joey got to stay home," Paul whined, snatching a carrot from the wrapped plate, then making a face at his sister. "Luce, how do you ruin carrots?"

Candace blinked. I watched her process his insult of her friend and her decision not to engage by a slow lowering of the lashes. "Joey has a science fair project to finish up, you do not," she said instead. Then she opened the screen door and practically shoved Karin and Harriet out into the cold sunshine. She slammed the girls' jackets into her husband's arms. "Find a place for these." Dismissed, he slinked off, carrying the jackets with him.

Lucy produced another drink. "How you didn't murder him during your childhood..." Candace sipped the drink, then smacked her lips.

"I didn't choose him," Lucy smiled.

Candace sighed. "I sometimes don't remember why I chose him, either."

Miriam leaned in as if about to receive some salacious gossip. "So, how's counseling going?"

Candace rolled her eyes heavenward. "We have been just the once. The counselor decided the next several visits will be individual so he can get the lay of the land."

I nodded. "It's a process."

Candace gave me a tight-lipped smile. "I can feel myself growing as a person already."

We watched silently while Jonas dragged the dog from the garage into a second back room in the house. The dog appeared to have some color around its muzzle and its paws scraped along the wooden floor as he unwillingly went.

Once the show was over, Miriam turned back to us. "How many kids are you expecting?"

Lucy pulled the covers off the food so Miriam would stop eyeballing it. "No idea."

"Is it a drop off party or an awkward parent small talk party?" I asked. The girls were turning seven. At this age, more parents were comfortable with their kids being watched by strangers, so they could go to the movies or shop in peace or whatever.

"Seven, it really could be anything," Candace said.

"Which is why you are here," Lucy said, plopping one of each type of appetizer into our waiting hands. "Taste these." She turned pointedly to Miriam. "Then fix them." After ensuring that we were going to comply with a sternly raised eyebrow, she dashed off to check on Danielle again.

Miriam cautiously took a nibble, made a hacking noise, and politely dusted the leftover crumbs into the garbage can. Candace shrugged and tossed hers back like a shot. Her grimace told me I should follow Miriam's lead. As Miriam rummaged through Lucy's depleted spice storage, Candace and I watched a number of sticky unaccompanied minors make their way to the backyard.

As Candace predicted, ultimately some parents stayed to hover over their young ones. These parents closely monitored their little angels' behavior toward other children, their breathing, and the ingredients Miriam pretended she hadn't added to the appetizers. Another set of parents slapped their cell phone numbers on post-it notes, affixed it to the front of the microwave, then hightailed it away from the chaos. We didn't have to interact with anyone.

About three mimosas in, Jonas was roused from his man-cave to play present delivery boy. Lucy photographed each child with the present they brought and the birthday girls. "For the thank-you notes," she explained. As if anyone else was organized enough to have their kids write thank-you notes. I did particularly enjoy the bugged out flash Lucy's eyes took on when Emily opened a present that was entirely filled with glitter glue.

Danielle and Emily got into a shoving match over the Pie in Face board game that was gifted to both of them from grandma in Jersey. Candace and I had to break it up before Pie-in-Face became Stomped-On-Mess. Danielle stomped up the stairs in a huff, creating little cracks in her brand new glittery plastic high heels. Emily led the charge on the ninja war, wielding a sawed off pool noodle like a saber. After that, Miriam was busy fussing over John's skinned knee. Candace begrudgingly held an icepack over Harriet's soon to be black eye, complaining about an upcoming dance recital picture that was now sure to elicit some tough questions. I barely stopped my dog poop covered son from entering the fray, but I wasn't fast enough to stop the dog from eating the cake.

Driving home afterward, Clifford patted my knee. "Good party. Not too chaotic." The sad thing was, he was serious. The whole time, he'd been sequestered with the boys while we had run our asses off doing crowd control. "Maybe we should do Becca's birthday at our house."

I snorted, "Hell no."

Me: How did you feel the task delegation went?
Lucy: He had one job.
Miriam: Two if you count the presents.
Lucy: The dog ate the cake.

Candace: This is why I don't give Paul any tasks.

Me: How else are they supposed to learn anything?

Lucy: What do you delegate to Clifford?

Me: Cooking.

Candace: I thought you said he couldn't cook.

Me: Neither can I.

Miriam: Bob is really wanting more responsibility. He's still mad at me about my mother.

Me: That might be something.

Miriam: What? Delegate the task of getting rid of my mother to Bob? She hates him.

Candace: Then that should be the perfect task for him.

Miriam: But how would we even do that? And I do still need her to babysit for me so it can't be permanent. I don't know guys. This sounds like another terrible idea.

Lucy: He could always find her a boyfriend.

Candace: That might actually work.

Bob very much enjoyed the suggestion of fixing up Miriam's mother. One of the sticking points of their marriage had always been Miriam's mother, Guadalupe. Bob knew it wasn't a fight he could ever win, but he wished that something could be done about Miriam's mother's involvement in their lives. While Miriam had always found her mother's distaste for Bob funny, lately it had been sapping her confidence in Bob as a father.

Which helped me learn something about circular arguments. Sometimes being patient with a person and allowing them to approach you with an idea for change is really the best idea. Or, in Miriam's case, let her pretend the idea wasn't Bob's.

Bob, being an extremely helpful sort, even offered to set up the dating website for Guadalupe. Miriam and her mother both refused his help with online dating apps. But Miriam did manage to get her to agree to a fix up, if it was made through the church.

Bob suggested men he knew at Guadalupe's church that might have things in common. "Your mother is into Soap Operas, cooking, gardening, criticizing me, and international soccer."

Miriam frowned, "Criticizing you? As a hobby?"

Bob shrugs.

Miriam decided to let that go. "So, who has those interests?"

"Mr. Wong?"

Miriam snorted. "Doesn't he hate you?"

"See, they already have a common interest."

"Do we know anything else about him?"

"He's a master gardener and has season tickets to the Nuggets."

"How do you know that?"

"I pay attention."

"You have been trying to get him to like you?"

"Maybe."

"Has it been working?"

"No." Bob sighed. "But this might."

"Why does he hate you?"

"He caught be barfing in his garden one morning after a walk with John."

"There's no recovering from that."

"Unless he falls in love."

"Love is really the answer?"

"Don't you think so?"

"How do we even get them together?"

Bob looked at Miriam suggestively. "You are the key. You need to let him know your mom is interested."

"But she isn't"

"But he doesn't know this."

"Does he speak Spanish?"

"Does it matter?"

"Yes."

"Then you should find this out, too."

"What are you going to do?"

"Annoy them both, so they have something to talk about."

"How self- sacrificing."

"I know."

Mr. Wong first spoke to Guadalupe one sunny morning after church when he overheard her swearing about how long Bob was taking to pull the car around. To the outside observer, she appeared to be admiring the roses budding outside of the chapel. True to his mission, Bob was taking an extraordinarily long time in order to annoy Miriam's mother. Mr. Wong found himself intrigued by this apparently sweet woman's colorful descriptions of a man Mr. Wong also personally disdained. He did in fact understand Spanish fluently, having gone with the church on a six-month mission to Guatemala in his late twenties. Keeping up with the language as best as he could through his working life, then as a retiree, he spent time volunteering in the local schools teaching English as a foreign language to Spanish-speaking children. It was part of the reason he was attracted to that particular church, was that it allowed him to keep up with his Spanish in as near native an environment as he could. Mr. Wong was a short, balding Chinese man who sometimes pretended to not speak English in order to annoy shopkeepers. "I planted those flowers last year," he said in Spanish by way of introduction to Guadalupe.

Embarrassed that he might have overheard her tirade about her son-in-law, Guadalupe gaped at the small man beside her, searching for a response. Finally, she came up with a response that ignored her rudeness altogether. "What color will they be when in bloom?"

"They are called Double Delight. They will have a red outside and mysterious yellow inside."

Guadalupe found her cheeks heating. Though his description had been completely innocuous, it also sounded romantic to her budding ear.

At that moment Bob did pull around and, seeing the two of them together, honked his horn instead of exiting the vehicle and assisting Guadalupe into the passenger side. She frowned at him darkly. Bob watched as Mr. Wong whispered something into Guadalupe's ear that had her laughing heartily. She shuffled to the passenger side of the car and slid herself into the seat. Miriam saved a secret smile for her husband in the review mirror.

Guadalupe rebuffed Miriam's attempts to help her pick out an outfit for their very first date. "It is not a date meja, it is a garden show." When Bob complimented Guadalupe's hat, she ran back to Miriam's bedroom to change.

After that first outing, it took Mr. Wong nearly two days to call Guadalupe again. The woman was so frantic, she was staring at her phone even when she was supposed to be watching John. Being the first one home from work, Bob immediately noticed her distress. He decided that instant to take Jimmy for a walk across Mr. Wong's front yard. He lingered out front of Mr. Wong's house long enough for the dog to water Mr. Wong's prized begonias. Mr. Wong followed him home in such a rage that Guadalupe came to the front yard to investigate what the fuss was about. The moment they saw each other, the tension was laughably apparent. Bob wasn't entirely sure what was said between them, but he observed the eye rolls and pointed looks that indicated it was something insulting to his person. Guadalupe followed Mr. Wong home, immediately forgetting her stared at cell phone and hungry grandson.

When he told Miriam about the incident later, she whooped with delight, and then worried that she might have to hire a babysitter to replace her mother.

Me: How did you decide which of your family members to leave the kids to in the will?

Candace: Morbid.

Lucy: I haven't got a will.

Miriam: I only have my mother.

Candace: I am just not planning on dying.

Me: But you've talked about it, right?

Candace: I am guessing Paul has his own ideas about the matter, but no, we haven't talked about it.

Me: You should have a plan.

Candace: Why? Are you trying to kill me and Paul off?

Lucy: I think this is another experiment. Guess what Paul is going to suggest, to see how wrong he is.

Me: No. Not an experiment. Just being practical.

Candace: No, I like this. If Paul and I are compatible, we will want the same thing for our children. If we aren't, then it is not meant to be.

Miriam: But you DO have children you have to decide about.

Candace: Pshaw. I told you I don't plan on dying, at least not at the same time as Paul. Tragedy.

Candace and Paul had gotten into the habit of driving in the same car to and from their counseling appointments. This way they had the rush hour traffic buffer of time to mentally prepare a game plan for their issues at counseling and then the driving home buffer of how they will continue to coexist after the appointment. It also meant that on this particular day, Candace was thinking about what I had said at lunch. The prospect of them dying. Together. And she was trying to figure out a way to broach the subject with the other member of the team.

Her death was a much more horrifying thought since she had left her children for that week. It had turned out so vastly different from how she thought it would, that she was now questioning whether she even had an impact on the children at all. What if they were all better off without her in their lives? If she left Paul, would they choose him? She shook her head at those dark thoughts. Yet another pressing matter: the thought of both of them dying at the same time. Since they were riding in a car together weekly over a congested long distance, the likelihood of them dying together had significantly increased over the previous years of their marriage. Was marriage counseling really increasing the likelihood of her children becoming orphans? Wouldn't they be best served by divorced parents who never spent any time together and therefore had no risk of dying at the same time, leaving them alone in the world? And how pissed would Candace be at spending her last moments on earth with Paul when she wasn't particularly happy with Paul?

All of these thoughts were swimming her head when she said to him, "If we are going to continue driving, we are going to have to pick godparents for our children."

Paul took his eyes off of the road to stare at her, befuddled and almost rammed into the back of a pickup truck. Candace screamed. He slammed on his brakes, swearing. "You see?"

Breathing heavily, he gripped the steering wheel. "No."

"We almost died." Candace's pulse was in her eardrum. "Just now."

"We did not almost die."

Was he not riding in the same car as her? Did he not just experience what she had? "We could have." She dragged her purse up from the footwell and clutched it to her chest. "And then who would our children go to?"

Paul roughly turned on the turn signal, then slid into another lane without checking his blind spot. "We would not care where they went because we would be dead."

Candace stared at him, unable to tell if he was being serious or not. "That's just like you. If it doesn't affect you, why worry about it?"

"Great. Another thing to work on in counseling." Paul turned the radio station volume up and began humming along to the rock band that was playing.

Candace fumbled with the radio dial to turn it back down, trying to bring back the subject at hand. "So, do you have an opinion about who we should leave them to? Your mother, right?"

Paul visibly shuddered. "Not that woman."

Candace was surprised. Though she didn't have much of a relationship with Paul's mother, she had assumed that he maintained contact with the hoity toity Jersey bitch. "Really, but I thought your upbringing made you the man you are today." She said, quoting one of his favorite acceptance speech lines. The medical community loved their Hero awards, so she had heard this speech rehearsed.

Paul shrugged, then sighed. "In the unlikely event of our deaths while our children are still young...."

"More likely now that we drive together."

Paul rolled his eyes. "In the unlikely event of our deaths, I think we should leave them to..." He was silent, so she looked up from rummaging in her purse for some gum. That telltale crease above his brow always indicated he was deep in thought. She'd been snapped at enough times to know the face for interrupting him. Finding the gum, she popped the piece in her mouth, swirling it around blankly. "I don't know. Your father, I suppose." He sounded doubtful.

Candace shuddered. "My father would not pay attention to them at all and lose them on the first outing." She loved her father. He was great fun for visits, but any real responsibility had never been his strong suit. She missed her own mother more than anything. Since her death, her father and been swimming along on charm it seemed.

"You dismissed my idea, which means you probably already have one of your own."

"Your sister," Candace said as soon as the idea popped into her head.

Paul snorted. "She would make mincemeat out of Harriet."

"I happen to love Lucy," Candace defended her friend staunchly.

"You can love Lucy, but do you love her parenting?" Paul challenged, taking another turn way too fast.

"You're suggesting my absent- minded father over your neo-nazi sister?"

"You said it."

Candace snorted. Paul laughed. It felt good when it hadn't felt good in a long while. "We are so screwed," he said.

Candace wrung her hands. Looking out the window to see how close they were to their destination, she idly watched a jogger at a crosswalk. "Don't tell her I called her a neo-nazi," she begged.

"I wouldn't tell her for fear she'd shoot me for it." He replied. Silence fell again in the car. The levity replaced with awkwardness. She missed the laughter, but didn't know what else to say. Thankfully Paul did, "Hey what about your other friends? It doesn't have to be a family member."

She was touched that he was still with her in this moment, when they could have easily let it fizzle. Candace considered. She always thought the children needed to stay in the family. The family knew the family traditions. But if the kids had godparents here, they could stay in their same schools, they would have friends. How had considering the logistics of her own death made her happier with her husband than anything they had done together in a long time?

They pulled up to the counselor's office at that moment, and Candace was pulled from her musings. She just couldn't afford to die right now.

Lesson learned: Sometimes getting the job done means just being on the same page.

Chapter 9

How to Insult Your Spouse Without Hurting Their Feelings

Candace: Jenna, you look skinny. What is your weight loss plan?

Lucy: Body positive, please.

Candace: That was body positive. I want to know her secret.

Miriam: Could you please refrain from dieting until the end of this pregnancy? I can't take being left out.

Me: I am not doing anything special.

Lucy: Beauty is just a construct, anyway.

Miriam: That's true, I just wish my construct didn't force me into a new bra size.

Candace: Well, Paul has been improving his beauty construct.

Lucy: How so?

Candace: He's dressing more casually and weight lifting.

Me: I thought counseling was going well.

Candace: It is.

Lucy: When a man improves his appearance, it means he is planning on being on the market.

Candace: Or he values my opinion.

Miriam: Did that sound genuine coming out of your mouth?

Candace: Oh God! Do I need to get a lawyer?

The male ego is a fickle thing. From the media coverage, we are taught that women lose value when they age. Gaining wrinkles, thin skin and shaky voices, while perfectly normal for the aging process, aren't attributes that lend credibility to women. It's different from the aging of men. When men gain wrinkles and grey hairs, they also gain prestige therefore become more distinguished with age. James Bond is a good example of a distinguished man that every woman is expected to want to fuck. As we age, we women need reassurances from our loved ones that we are still fuckable as well. This need for reassurance is so well documented in the media that many male partners do it naturally.

Living in close proximity with a man, you learn that not every man thinks he is James Bond. And that both partners in the relationship need reassurance of their attractiveness from time to time. Giving these reassurances to our male partners has been somewhat of a challenge because male insecurity isn't so well documented in the media. Take Valentine's Day, for instance. What the heck is a woman supposed to give her male valentine for this Hallmark holiday? Flowers? A teddy bear?

Giving compliments needed to be something we actively tried on our partners. Lucy unwittingly paved the way for us as she prepped for her most recent date night.

***

Jonas had been in the bathroom for over a half an hour. Lucy was lying on the bed, casually surfing her phone. The girls were at a play date and they had dinner plans. Lucy had been ready to leave for a while but Jonas hadn't come out yet. She knew he wasn't pooping because that had already disrupted their breakfast routine. She was starting to wonder if he was masturbating in preparation for their date, but she didn't have the nerve to go in there and find out.

When the fifteen minute alert on her phone went off, she knew she would have to intercede or they would miss their reservation. Cautiously, she slid the bathroom door open and poked her head inside. At first, she couldn't figure out what she was seeing. The details slowly came into focus until her brain processed the whole. Jonas was plastered up against the mirror, his face contorted in an awkward grimace as he carefully angled her metal tweezers inside of a nostril.

"What are you doing?" she breathed.

"Ow Fuck," he dropped the tweezers into the sink, clutching his nose. "You distracted me," he complained from behind his hand.

"I have been waiting for thirty minutes for you to come out of here."

He blinked at her sheepishly. "I found hairs."

"Congratulations, you're a mammal," Lucy said drily, one hand on a hip.

Jonas leaned back toward the mirror, carefully removing his hand in order to examine his nostril. "Luce, I have my dad's nose hairs. I am too young to have my dad's nose hairs."

Lucy blinked at him, unsure of how to proceed. She was getting pretty hungry and knew that if she said the wrong thing in this moment, her ability to acquire food would be significantly delayed.

Silently, she watched him palpate the skin around his nose and chin. "Do you think I look my age?"

Lucy clutched her stomach. Now, he wanted to have an existential crisis, now? When she finally had a moment free to eat something not related to chicken fingers? "What is age, really?" she tried.

Jonas turned back to her, his hands dropping from his face, revealing pink puffy flesh where he had prodded the surface. Lucy schooled her features to keep from re-vealing any negative emotion that would delay her meal further. "Lucy, I look like someone's father."

Really, that was just too much for her. "You ARE someone's father," she said blandly.

"But no one wants to fuck someone's father."

"You have to fuck in order to become someone's father."

Jonas pouted. "You know what I mean."

Impatient now, Lucy didn't moderate her tone at all. "No, Jonas, I really don't. We were planning on fucking after we fucking ate dinner."

"Were?" he squeaked, latching on to the most impor-tant word from her sentence.

"If you don't feed me, I will not be in the mood," she complained.

Realizing that his existential crisis might come in the way of a sure thing. Jonas pulled his metaphorical big boy pants on, stopped staring at his own reflection in the mirror, and took his wife to dinner.

***

Miriam made a frustrated growl. Bob heard it as he walked by the bathroom. Still wanting to prove his value to the household after the vacation, he forced himself to inquire, "Do you need any help?"

"I am embarrassed to ask," came the muffled reply.

"Miriam, we are about to have a second child together. There shouldn't be anything left to be embarrassed about." Bravely, Bob entered the bathroom.

He found Miriam stark naked in a squatting position, hovering over a hand mirror on the floor. Bob blinked a few times, unsure what he was seeing.

"I can't reach," she moaned.

Bob scratched his head, clearing his throat. "What can't you reach?"

Miriam stood up and then plopped herself onto the closed lid of the toilet, defeated. "I am trying to groom myself."

"Groom?"

Continuing on without hearing him, Miriam's eyes began to fill with big fat tears. "My stupid belly is so big that I can't see what I am doing."

"What are you doing?"

She looked at him through her tears now running down her cheeks. "Grooming. Weren't you listening?"

"What is grooming?" he asked, pulling her into his arms, making shushing noises.

"Of course, you wouldn't know anything about hair maintenance. You hairy beast."

"Ouch."

"Oh, don't be offended. I like your hair."

"Do you? Or do you just tolerate it because it is stuck all over me?"

Miriam rolled her eyes. "I like your hair."

"Say it like you mean it."

"I do. I like running my hands through the hair on your chest."

"But what about the hair on my butt?"

"That too."

"Really?"

"Really," she insisted. "And your hair is really not the point. Mine is."

"I don't mind a little hair on you either," he said consolingly.

"Oh, this maintenance is not for you."

Now Bob was offended. "It's not? Who else will be seeing it?"

Miriam rubbed her face against the cool cotton of his shirt front. "The doctors."

Bob chuckled. Hearing that, she punched him pretty hard, and he had to muffle a grunt of pain.

"Don't laugh at me. I thought it was considerate that since they were all going to be down there for the birth, that I should keep things nice and manicured."

"Did you do this last time?"

"Last time I didn't have another child home with me all day and scheduled it to be done by a professional," she wailed.

A little more this day, the mysteries of womanhood were revealed to Bob. Bob was, however, made of stern stuff. He might even be able to make this work to his benefit. "I am not a licensed professional, but I do have enough body hair of my own to qualify for competence."

She frowned at him, then hiccupped a little. "Are you offering to trim my Concha for me?"

He wiggled his eyes suggestively. "I promise it won't hurt unless you want it to."

She laughed. Then she cried. Then she bent backward and let the man work.

When he had finished, she admired the handiwork in the mirror. It had taken longer than the professional visits she remembered. It did not have the straight lines or evenness that she would have gotten from a professional job. Miriam wisely refrained from criticizing. What he lacked in skill, he made up for in eagerness. "How come your back isn't this well trimmed?" she asked.

She was lucky he had already unplugged the trimmers by this point.

***

Once their food was in front of them, Lucy should have known that Jonas would not let the matter drop. "You don't tell me I am attractive anymore."

Mouth full, Lucy raised a single eyebrow. "Is that a requirement?"

Jonas dabbed at his mouth with a napkin. "It would be nice."

She ran her eyes up and down his body in what she hoped was a hungry look. The effect was ruined by a lady like burp. "You know what's hot, Jonas?" she leaned in close to him over the dimly lit table.

Eagerly, he leaned in to meet her. "What?"

"When you do what I tell you, when I tell you to do it."

Jonas leaned back. "I want to be wanted for more than my ability to please you."

Lucy sighed, then rolled her eyes. "Fine. I like your butt."

"Was that so hard?" He smiled smugly, giving a little satisfied wiggle in his seat.

"You know Jonas, usually it is the woman needing re-assurance about her appearance."

She watched him take a big juicy bite of the Italian meatball sandwich he had ordered and dribbled down his chin. It wasn't disgusting, more like the person she loved was sitting across from her at the table. It was familiar and comfortable just being together. That was what she liked best about this whole marriage thing. "You don't need reassurance, though. You're so hot, you could leave me at any second," he said.

She smiled. Then she leaned across the table so far that she could nibble the sauce off of his skin. "Is that what this is about? That I am so much hotter than you?" She appreciated the little hitch in his breath he gave.

He leaned closer so that he could kiss her back. "Yeah. I just can't wrap my mind around why you would want a schmo like me."

She snatched his sandwich from his plate to take her own juicy bite. Shrugging, she explained, "I love all of you, from your taste in sandwiches, to your way with the girls, to your attention to detail."

"Don't forget my adoration of your body."

"How could I forget that?"

He raised some eyebrows suggestively. "Want me to adore it some more up close?"

"No," she said, and continued eating the rest of his sandwich.

***

"Come on Jenna, just eat a little bit more." He waved a fork covered in gelatinous material in front of my mouth as if I were a recalcitrant child that needed a pretend airplane to open my mouth.

"I am truly not hungry, Clifford," I said.

"But I made it special for you." He had remembered something I said about liking chicken marsala with extra cheese. The exact circumstance of that discussion was in front of a coworker who I didn't want to offend. It had no basis for food I actually wished to consume.

I smacked my lips. "And I ate it, even if it did taste like sawdust." We had been married so long that Clifford's forays into cooking and my commentary only served to help him improve, rather than insult him.

"Remember when I made you that lamb dish?"

I closed my eyes in a pained grimace. I remembered all too well. The handmade mint jelly. It made the meat cold. "I never told you I hated lamb."

I opened my eyes to a smug sparkle in his own eyes. "I knew that. I just wanted you to admit that."

"In all fairness, if I liked lamb at all, I would have liked that dish."

"No, you wouldn't have," he sighed.

I agreed, laughingly. "You're right." I dabbed at my lips, then carefully took a sip of water. "You would think your cooking would improve over time with practice."

He shrugged. "I guess it's not meant to be."

"I know you're just trying to fatten me up for your own nefarious purposes." I said.

He got up and traveled to the other side of the table to take me into his arms and kiss my neck. Cupping my shrunken breasts in his hands, he said, "You've got me. I would much prefer to drown in these things."

I rolled my eyes. "Sorry to disappoint."

"I will have to survive on the meager scraps you give me." Kissing him, I patted his butt as he slid back into his chair. The kids were sacked out in front of the television, having eaten dinner in rapid scoops into their gaping mouths, then begging to be allowed more television before bed. Clifford was going out with some coworkers, so I was counting down to some quiet time of my own after the kids' bedtime.

He picked up our plates to put them on the side of the sink. "Ok, I guess I am heading out now." I really loved my husband, but I also really loved my husband being gone so I could guilt free watch that serial killer documentary I had been saving. I blinked at him lovingly while suddenly taking notice of his appearance, an untucked kitty unicorn t-shirt and mussed graying hair sporting a sparkly purple barrette compliments of our daughter. "Omigod, you cannot wear that out."

"How often do you actually look at me?" He cocked his head to the side.

"Apparently not often enough." I got up from the table to begin scrubbing the dishes.

"I have been wearing this all evening."

"I look at you."

"Did you notice my haircut?"

What was I supposed to say to that? No, of course I didn't notice his hair cut. His hair looked the exact same as it had yesterday. It never changed. I glared at him suspiciously. He could have been testing me. Maybe he didn't actually get a haircut and was seeing if I would lie about it. I wouldn't put dirty schemes past Clifford.

I decided to change the subject instead. I pulled the barrette out of his hair, showing it to him. He grinned. "Go change your shirt, at least."

"What's wrong with my shirt?"

"Its not very professional."

Clifford sighed, grabbing a dish from me and placing it into the dishwasher. "It is drinks with coworkers. I don't have to be professional."

"Don't you care what they think of you?" I asked, handing him another one.

"Nope." Such a man's way of thinking and yet I totally believed that he actually didn't care if his coworkers made fun of him for his t-shirt choice.

I turned to him and glanced up and down at his lanky frame. "Do you care what I think of you?"

He kissed me. "To a point."

I swatted at him, but he was already backing away toward the garage, laughing. "How did I get stuck with such a cocky spouse?"

"Just lucky I guess."

***

True to his word, Paul had been home more often in the evenings, since he had moved back in. He'd been using some of his free time in the evening to weight lift. Sometimes Joey even joined him.

This evening, Candace was dressed in her favorite pant suit for a political book opening. She climbed the stairs to the attic to remind Paul that she was leaving. Joey was crouched in the corner surfing his iPad while his red-faced father heaved the 50 pound free weights in a slow arc. Candace watched the vein in his neck pulse uncomfortably with the effort.

Objectively, Paul was a handsome man. Candace tried to imagine his large hands on her body. It had been so long that she honestly couldn't remember how it felt. What would it be like to kiss him? Would she recognize him, or would the smell of his breath and the feel of his skin instantly repel her? This was definitely not the time to be having these thoughts with her son in the room and a client waiting on her arrival. She cleared her throat because, while she had been in this door way watching both males for several minutes, neither had acknowledged her presence. "I am leaving you in charge of bedtime."

Paul grunted as he set the weights down at his feet and rubbed his face with his bare hands. Through a couple of gasps, he managed to get a coherent sentence out. "Where are you going again?"

Candace frowned. "I told you. The press secretary's tell all book release party."

Paul frowned, looking around for a towel. Seeing it near the door, she scooped it up with her bare foot and then tossed it in his direction, afraid to get too close to sweaty man. He might drip on her silk. "I know you told me. I just forgot."

Candace sighed. "So are you going to be ok handling the girls?"

"No Candace. I am going to feed them sugar and let them watch YouTube all night."

Candace bit her lip. "Joey, did you finish your homework?"

Joey didn't look up from his device. "Yeah Mom, just go alright?"

Candace was overwhelmed by the love she felt emanating from her two guys. They deserved each other.

Paul bent to retrieve a plastic glass of water before facing her again. He scanned her. "You're wearing a pantsuit. I am guessing the press secretary is also wearing a pantsuit?"

"Yes. Not that it's any of your business what she is wearing tonight, but we are both wearing pantsuits. What is wrong with that?" Candace challenged.

"Why do all women in politics wear pant suits? It's not like the rest of the world doesn't know you are a female."

Candace's mouth fell open. "I happen to like this suit."

"Because it makes you feel as powerful as a man?" He leaned on the wall near her, but just out of reach.

Candace's fingers itched to slap lie down. "All I am saying is that I know this woman has aspirations for a presidential bid and I think people would take her more seriously if she acted like a woman."

"And how do women act?" Candace seethed.

He flexed as he reached up for his bar. "Soft, sweet, helpful."

"You must think I am not much of a woman then, as I am never any of those."

Paul grunted, lowering the bar. "Indeed, you are not."

"Well, it's nice to know that you are confident enough to be married to someone who doesn't act like a real woman."

He grunted again.

Candace checked her watch. Already five minutes behind schedule, she certainly did not have enough time to change before leaving. What did he know, anyway?

Lesson Learned: Appreciate what you've got when you've got it.

Chapter 10

Dating Your Spouse is Just Taking an Interest in That Thing They're Into

The unexpected consequences of our week away from our husbands was that they all suddenly wanted to spend time with us. I think it was a counterattack for the experiments we were concocting on them. We really should have stopped allowing them to communicate.

Miriam: Bob started watching Outlander with me and now he wants to read the books.
Candace: Omigod. They are invading.

Lucy: How would they feel if we started doing their activities?

Candace: Paul doesn't have activities. He works and reads medical journals.

Lucy: He goes to the gym.

Candace: Is that where he goes when I am carting the children to their activities on the weekend?

Me: Outlander is a good show.

Miriam: I know. We cannot wait until next season.

Lucy: He really likes watching it? He's not just doing it for you.

Miriam: He definitely likes it. He made me promise not to watch the last two episodes without him.

Miriam, an avid romance novel enthusiast, was very excited at the debut of her favorite romance novel on Primetime. So excited, in fact, that she taught herself to make haggis and steamed cabbage. She served it to Bob and herself that very night. After throwing most of their dinner down the drain, Miriam eagerly took the remote in hand and prepared to be enchanted by Outlander. Bob put their son to bed, then prepared to surf the news on his phone while mindlessly rubbing his pregnant wife's swollen feet.

Much to Bob's horror, he also found himself sucked into the turbulent world of ancient Scotland and the tale of Claire and Jamie's budding romance. After three episodes, Miriam had to pull out her copy of the book for reference to answer his probing questions. Miriam later bought a fan-fic book about a couple who had traveled to Scotland to visit all of the places mentioned in the book. She offered to have Bob read it, but fan fiction was a bridge too far. He did agree that a trip to Scotland might improve his golf game.

It became a thing for them to enjoy together. She even bought him a Jamie Fraser faced hoodie, which he refused to wear anywhere.

Then Bob had to leave for a business trip during the final two episodes of the first season. He made Miriam promise to wait to watch the episodes until he got back. She said, "I will pine for you like Claire pined for Jamie." That really should have been a sign. Spoiler alert: Claire marries another man in the future.

Bob left for Sacramento, leaving Miriam alone at the house. The second to last episode aired on a dark and stormy night. Miriam, alone with nothing to focus on, became agitated. What if she didn't set the recording right? What if the episode was too violent and censors pulled it from the air, never to be viewed again? She tried to stay strong by doing an approximation of Lamaze breathing she vaguely remembered from her first childbirth experience. Lightning flashed outside of the house. She picked up the remote to confirm that the recording was set up correctly. Then she flipped to a Spanish dubbed Baking show. The rain on the rooftop was so fierce that she had to increase the volume on the tv set. She picked up her phone to check the weather, which led her to surf some Outlander fan sites. Just a few. As the comments on the episode crawled across her screen, her fingers began to twitch. She had to see what they were talking about.

She flicked the remote to the channel just in time for the last notes of the opening song to fade to a finish. She watched the whole episode. She laughed. She cried. She glanced at the empty couch cushion next to her. Then the guilt set in. She hugged her knees to her chest. What was she going to do? She had broken a promise to Bob. She ticked the cursor over the episode she'd just finished. The red line at the bottom glaringly denouncing her violation of trust. What would Bob think? If she couldn't remain faithful to their tv show, how could she claim to be a faithful partner in life? She may as well have cheated on him. She rubbed her swollen belly for comfort.

She could fix this. She just needed to hide her tracks. She cued up the episode again from the recording, then clicked on the replay episode option. It still claimed to be previously viewed. She checked other air times to record a future time that she wouldn't watch. Sadly, the next scheduled time was after Bob returned from his trip. Stupid television executives and their stupid scheduling. She flung the remote to the coffee table in disgust. The remote landed on its face. To this day Miriam would never know what button was pressed, however the deed was done. The episode was deleted.

Bob arrived home later the following week. Miriam nervously met him at the airport. She made him his favorite meal, then rubbed his feet after putting the kid to bed. Anyone paying attention at this point would have suspected that Miriam was hiding something. Bob didn't. Bob thought she was happy to see him.

He cued up the television to the latest unwatched episode of Outlander. The one Miriam had managed not to watch because she had come to my house to hide. The episode opened with a description of all the violence and lovemaking that was the previous episode. Miriam burst into tears. "I cheated on you, Bob," she sobbed.

Bob, who had been reaching to comfort his teary hormonal wife, stopped mid lean, scarcely remembering to pause the episode. He sat back from her, tucking his hands beneath him. He regarded his wife as if he had never met her before. "How? You've been so queasy."

Miriam hiccupped. "It was dark, and I was so lonely. I went on the internet..." she trailed off, at a loss to explain.

"The internet. Miriam?" Bob sighed bewildered. "I was only gone two weeks."

"I know." She sobbed, her cheeks pinkening. "I am a horrible person."

Bob looked at her for a long time. "Well, do you want a divorce?" He said finally in a very reasonable sounding Bob voice.

"You're going to divorce me over this?" she shrieked. Latina fire bloomed in cheeks that were covered in snot and tears. "I'll have you know that Frank never divorced Claire."

Bob leaned forward at his own risk to cover his wife's mouth with his hand as gently as he could. "Claire traveled back in time, Miriam, it is not the same thing."

"If I could travel back in time, I would take it back," she grumbled. "Divorce? What kind of man are you?"

Bob shook his head, leaning away from her glare, and pinning her with one of his own. He considered himself a reasonable guy, but come on. There had been no signs of this. "Did you do it in my bed?"

"What difference does it make where?"

He pressed a hand to his forehead. "I am really trying to be reasonable here, Miriam."

She crossed her arms across her ample chest mutinously. "If you must know, it was right here on the couch." Bob looked down at his cushion, horrified. Her face softened, then crumbled, and she was back to sobbing again. "I tried to cover it up, so you wouldn't find out what I had done, but I just deleted the recording."

"There was a recording?" Bob goggled.

"Of course there was. Millions of people were probably recording it at the same time that they were watching it."

"Well, I wasn't one of them." Bob frowned.

"I know. And I am sorry."

"Sorry? Miriam, what about our son?" Bob leaned forward to shake her. She gripped his hands on her shoulders and he let go.

"He was in bed. He's not old enough to watch it."

Bob sputtered. "I should say he's not old enough to watch his mother's sex tape," Bob shouted.

Miriam's jaw dropped. "What are you talking about? You love Outlander. It is not pornography."

Bob stood up from the couch to pace. "Why are you talking about Outlander at a time like this?" he shouted again.

Miriam stood up too. The better to shout from her diaphragm. "I was always talking about Outlander. What were you talking about?"

"Your confession of cheating on me with another man right here on the couch."

"I watched the episode of Outlander by myself. There was no other man," she screamed. "And then I deleted it." She really had to punch that home because he was being so unreasonable about this.

Bob burst out laughing and slumped to the couch. He wrapped his arms around his wife and yanked her into his lap. He kissed the side of her neck. Which she let him do because she was very confused that they were suddenly not fighting anymore. "I don't care that you watched it without me," he said into her neck.

"Then what were we fighting about?"

Lucy: Jonas came to yoga last week.

Candace: I wish I had seen that.

Me: He can't do that. That's your thing.

Lucy: I know. He gave me some line about how he was doing it to get closer to me.

Me: How did it go?

Lucy: Well, he came to Bikram Intense core class.

Me: So he fainted.

Lucy: I could have sold tickets and popcorn.

Jonas was free on a Tuesday after lunch. After Bob had told him about the infidelity scare, he decided that his own wife could use some checking up on. After all, Lucy was a beautiful woman. More beautiful than a schmo like him deserved. He knew that she spent every afternoon before school pick up at the yoga studio in the mall. He had known a number of second wives to be former yoga instructors. This might be how they met them.

Being a fairly scrawny, hairless man, he opted to wear a swimshirt and sweatpants to his wife's yoga studio. When he checked in at the front desk, the skinny red head took his information, then scanned her eyes up and down his body. She grinned. "Do you need to rent a mat?" she asked between pops of her gum. He always thought people looked like cows chewing their cud when they did that.

He leaned toward her flirtily. "I don't know, do I?"

"You do." Blinking, she handed him a thick gray spongy bit of plastic rolled tight. "You better get in there to stretch a little before class begins."

Jonas nodded his thanks, then slung the mat over his shoulder to enter the room. He wondered why he would need to stretch before a stretching class. Yoga was, after all, glorified stretching to hypnotic music.

Stepping through the door to the studio was like stepping off of a plane into Florida, in July, in the swampy part. He felt smacked with air being sucked from his lungs in wet, sopping gasps. He glanced at the now closed door, thinking how sturdy it was to have been able to contain a different weather pattern within a room.

Jonas looked around the room for an empty place to park his mat. He chose a spot near the back window next to the vent. Glancing at the other occupants in the room, he appreciated the broad expanses of bare skinned muscular forms displayed by the women. A guy could get used to this sensory feast. He did love yoga pants, and these women made them better by barely covering anything else.

One woman was bent in half, pressing her perky bottom up into the air. So this was what he had been missing. The room was dotted here and there by a couple of men, also stripped down to nearly nothing. What body hair they had was so manicured that he was convinced they were gay.

A blonde woman unrolled her mat beside his. She was so voluptuous that her breasts spilled out of the top of her sports bra like mounds of bread dough. He was certain she couldn't be a regular and vowed to do better on the poses than her. Next he watched as a rail thin brunette bounced in to the room on ballerina toes preceded by his own wife. She gaped at him before moving to the unoccupied mat directly in front of his own. He was now extremely grateful for his sweatpants that could hide his hard on when he watched his wife bend over in front of him for the next hour.

Within five minutes, however, Jonas was not able to maintain enough blood pressure to adequately inflate a hard on. The steam in the room melted down his throat. It took all of his concentration to stare at a spot on the wall that would keep him from falling on his face, tangled in his own limbs. His supposedly waterproof swim shirt was now dripping from the ten pounds of sweat that had escaped his pores. The perky brunette kept yelling commands in a husky drill sergeant voice. "Yes, you can. Don't tell yourself no." She wanted him to put his foot where?

Finally, the balance exercises ended, and they moved to the floor. Although, after dripping all of that sweat, the floor didn't feel quite so steady. His wife executed a perfect headstand while his flailing cock didn't even stir an acknowledgement. His ears began to ring with the effort of keeping one foot from sliding out from under him. He pulled off the shirt, letting it fall to the ground with a messy plop. He would have removed his pants, but he needed them to cradle his foot next to his groin. The brunette came over to assist him. He tried to tell her that he was too sweaty to touch, when she cracked something in his back. That sent him deeper into the pose, freeing his lungs from his rib cage with a sudden whoosh of air. He lost his grip with his hands, both sets of fingers parting ways like reality tv show stars after a fight. His cheek connected with the soggy mat and he lay there, staring toward his wife's ass. She grinned at him. He was filled with an immense relief, almost like he'd been brought closer to understanding something significant about life. Maybe he'd come back next week too.

Me: Clifford wants to come with us to 90s night dance party.
Lucy/Candace: No way.
Lucy: He will totally ruin the vibe.
Me: What vibe? We go there to dance.
Candace: We go there to have drinks bought for us.
Me: He said he would buy the drinks.
Lucy: Can he dance?
Me:
Miriam: I think it's cute that he wants to come.
Me: I don't like to park downtown, anyway. This way, we have a chauffeur.

Clifford dances like Billy Crystal in When Harry met Sally, all teeth and gangly arms and frizzy hair. He dances like he doesn't care who is watching. He has no rhythm to speak of, so when he tries to dance with a partner, they end up rocking into each other or getting an elbow to the chin.

At 90s night, he made good on the offer to chauffeur us and buy us drinks. He called himself our chaperone, proclaiming that he wouldn't leave us alone to the wolves, no matter how much we wanted him to. At least three hopeful twenty somethings had been dry humped by Clifford before slinking away from our dance circle.

Miriam was laughing and twirling with her hands in the air to most songs, even the rap ones. Candace, Lucy and I were scowling. Clifford looked like a stud. We looked taken. With our marital status, went the gossip and party atmosphere that generally attended these events. My well -meaning husband had no clue how much we wanted him to fall and injure himself right then, so he would leave the dance floor.

I was not sure what we expected to get out of a night of dancing, but it wasn't this. We are four middle-aged women, mothers, in a nightclub and we had never felt more out of place than that night. I suppose in some small way, bumping against strangers on a dance floor gave us some sort of confirmation that we were still attractive. That we were still young. That if Clifford were to die, I might be able to find someone else to love me. Which is crazy. I love Clifford. Well, I don't love Clifford when he spins on his head like a 90s hip hop star. Youch. I don't need to find someone else to love me because Clifford loves me. That should be enough. Candace's face as Clifford booty shook his way to the bar said she felt the wrongness too.

We were all disappointed when he came back cheerfully holding up a pink business card. "Hey, I got a phone number." Fucking men and their ability to age beautifully.

Me: So the men are clearly revolting.

Lucy: Especially Clifford's dance moves.

Miriam: Did he call that number?

Me: No, he did not.

Candace: My therapist says that Paul and I should do something together.

Lucy: You see how well that has worked out for us. Jonas bought a ten pack for the studio.

Candace: You should be so proud.

Lucy: I am.

Miriam: You could find a tv show you both enjoy.

Me: What does Paul enjoy?

Candace: I don't know.

Lucy: Don't you think that might be a problem?

Candace: It hasn't been before now.

Miriam: What did you used to do together before you had kids?

Candace: Drink and have sex.

Me: You still like to do that.

Candace: Paul stopped drinking when all of the statistics came out about doctors and their drinking problems.

Me: You should find out what Paul likes to do now.

Candace: How am I supposed to find that out?
Lucy: You could ask him.

Paul was drying the dishes later that night, handing them to Candace to put away. It was strangely a peaceful way to pass the evening. The television was off and the kids were upstairs in their rooms. Candace had this strange feeling of nervousness in her chest. Like the butterflies one feels when you have coerced a moment alone with a crush and now have to confess your feelings. Candace wasn't sure if a husband counted as a crush, and she had no idea what her feelings were for this person, even after several weeks of therapy. So far, what she did know was that they were not intimate enough for sex and that Paul really didn't know the definition of intimacy. Juliet, their counselor, had suggested spending time together to bring up the intimacy, and Paul had taken that to mean that when they were alone, he should touch Candace more often. Little brushes of his hands on her neck or shoulder. Sometimes his fingers would tangle with hers while they were walking next to each other. Each of these things sent shudders of revulsion through Candace, who viewed them as forced attempts at normalcy but not genuine acts of affection. It was as if Juliet had given Paul a map back to Candace and Paul was following it place by place, but not taking in any of the scenery or enjoying the journey. It all felt very wrong.

Candace had promised Juliet that she would try. She adopted what she hoped was not a grimace on her face. "Did you hear Jonas is taking up yoga with Lucy?"

She watched a small twitch appear on the corner of his mouth. Did that count as a smile? Did it look like her forced attempts? "Clifford might have said something."

"Clifford huh? You two talk?"

Paul set his dish down in order to give Candace his full attention. "Is there a law that says I can't?"

Candace scrunched her forehead, looking for the trap in his question. "No." She turned away from him to grab a glass to quench her suddenly parched throat. "I just didn't know you were friends."

"It's a recent thing," he said cryptically.

Candace squared her shoulders and persisted toward her goal. "Anyway, the girls and I were talking and a lot of the guys were trying things with their wives and I thought we might... try... something," she ended lamely.

Paul cocked an eyebrow at her suggestively. "Something?"

Candace stepped back, shaking her head. "Something, I don't know."

Paul leaned forward, chuckling warmly. "You are really bad at this."

Candace gaped at him like a fish. "At what?"

"Asking me out."

"I shouldn't have to ask you out," she grumbled. "We are married."

"Are we?"

She cocked her head to the side, consideringly. She took in the casual shirt sleeves rolled up, the bare feet, the mostly done shared chore, the house they maintained together. "I can't think of another definition for it."

"Yes Candace, I would love to go out with you," he said mockingly. "I have been waiting with bated breath for you to ask me."

"You don't have to be sarcastic about it."

"Excuse me if I am a little sarcastic as I can't count how many times I have been shut down over the last couple of years asking you to things." She noticed that he was breathing heavily, as if stressed. Funny, she didn't think she did that to him anymore.

"Well then, you must be incredibly bad at it because I can't recall a single time when you asked me out in the last decade," she retorted.

This time, it was his turn to gape at her. She held his stare, not saying anything. There was tension between them, but not the sexual kind. It was tired and raw with so much baggage she didn't know if she had it in her to unpack it all or if she should just pick up and move on without it.

He blinked. "Fine. Let's do this."

"I thought you'd already said yes." She shut the dishwasher turned away from him to pick up the shoes and jackets littering the hallway. "What are you into these days? We should do something you like." She suggested, trying to be a good partner.

"I have been meaning to tryout the Krav Maga studio."

"What is that?"

"You'll see," he said ominously.

****

He had told her to wear something loose that she could move in. She had googled Krav Maga when he was getting his shoes on. She was actually getting excited about this. According to Wikipedia, Krav Maga was a military self defense fighting system developed for the Israeli Defense forces. The only other site she had time to check out promised that she "would be the best version of herself ever!"

It was Friday night, she'd actually gotten me to watch the kids. Something about testing out godliness. The two of them were off like two awkward teenagers that were suddenly, irrevocably alone. Luckily, the silent drive to the studio was a short one. They were soon taking their positions among a group of widely varied sized people in a gym that smelled of sweat socks and cumin. The instructor was a lean, forceful, short man with a black curly Jew-fro and a thick New York accent.

Candace felt her blood rush through her ears as she struggled to follow the movements he demonstrated. She concentrated on her body and not what the others might be seeing of her body. She whispered to herself, I will be the best version of myself.

As she moved through the positions, her muscles warmed up and began to hum with the rhythms she recognized from the fitness classes she'd met Lucy in. She was aware of every part of herself in a way she hadn't been in a while.

The instructor began each phase of movement with a story that demonstrated when the movement would be useful in real life. As each person tried the move, the instructor moved through the room, adjusting postures here and there. Candace, like an overeager student, drank in his praise of her balance. She was feeling like this could be their regular thing when the instructor cued them for a drink break before the next phase of the class.

She hopped over to Paul, taking in his glistening, lean form objectively. She could recognize that he was still a relatively attractive man. She tried a smile at him to see how it felt. Not too weird. She hadn't really been paying attention to him at all in the class until this point. "How is it going for you?"

He shrugged. "Just about what I thought."

"So you like it?" By his tone, she really couldn't tell.

The instructor cued them to partner up for the next part. The person she came with seemed the obvious choice. This time the instructor had an assistant that he had help him demonstrate the tackle that he wanted the pairs to try. She would have to let Paul approach her aggressively and practice the motion they had been learning on him as defense. When it was actually their turn to try the move, Paul looked at her cautiously before beginning. He waited for her to acknowledge that she knew he would be threatening her. She nodded for him to approach. He moved his large form into her space, intimidatingly stepping a wide foot forward. With a sweep of his other foot, they were sharing the same air. His face was close, too close. She knew she wasn't supposed to back down, but she couldn't get her brain to remember the moves her limbs were supposed to make. He was big. Bigger than she'd realized. The hairs on the back of her neck tingled. She remembered feeling this way when he cornered her on the stairs that day that Harriet had learned to tie her shoes.

Her ears filled with white noise and her forehead grew fuzzy. Released from their paralysis, her limbs moved of their own accord in a movement that was too natural to be the correct one she'd practiced for the single class. Paul was down on the mat before she knew what had happened. Clutching his left cheek. She had punched him.

Embarrassingly, the assistant came by to check on them. The assistant hoisted Paul off of the mat and into a chair and left them at the back of the room while she got him an icepack. Candace was still reeling from her reaction. She had no explanation for what had come over her. It was as if her body had taken control of her mind. And now that she was back in command, she took in Paul's slumped form and couldn't feel regret. She apologized anyway. The mane was obviously hurt. "Shit. I am sorry."

"You should be. I have a presentation tomorrow." He groaned behind closed hands.

Emotion bubbled up in her throat, threatening to choke her. This man she had born children with didn't know her, didn't even seem to like her. A normal person would have tried asked something about her mental state instead of laying blame. But Paul wasn't a caring partner and as she looked back, he had never been. He'd been a handsome mistake. Mistakes could be fixed. "I want a divorce."

Lesson learned: You don't have to enjoy every activity your spouse enjoys to be a good partner.

Chapter 11

The Unconditional Love of Dogs and Babies

Candace: I need to get a dog.

Me: Why?

Candace: I need something that will love me unconditionally.

Miriam: Your children love you.

Candace: Not anymore. Not now that I am divorcing their father.

Lucy: Oh Candy. I still love you.

Candace: You may be the only one who understands.

Me: The love of a dog. Hmm....

Candace: Stop writing and actually talk to us, Jenna.

Me: I was thinking of a good response.

Miriam: I think we need to go to the hospital now.

Me: There's nothing wrong with my brain just because I am thinking.

Miriam: I wasn't talking about you Jenna.

Lucy: Oh!

Candace: Oh!

Miriam: Someone needs to go get Bob.

I went to go get Bob. Even though I was dizzy and actually wasn't feeling all that great. The new medication I was on was causing some weird side effects. I was counting on adrenaline to get me and Bob safely to the hospital and then I could rest.

I glanced at him, clutching the seat nervously. Miriam's mother had arrived at their house to stay with John just as I had arrived to pick up Bob. Bob didn't do well with barf, blood, or in a crisis involving his wife. It had been agreed on early that his responsibility was to bring the hospital bag and not die in transit. They had made this arrangement because: 1) Bob had crashed the car on the way to the birth of their son, and 2) Miriam's Dad had left on the day of her birth so she was weird about making sure Bob could make it to the hospital for their child's birth.

Candace and Lucy had taken her to the hospital immediately upon realizing that her water broke. This was not at all like the first time, which consisted of hours of labor in a cool, incensed room. Second children rarely got the same treatment, anyway. Lucy regaled her with her war story of birthing twins while Candace drove, obeying all traffic laws, and wincing slightly as Miriam cursed her to speed up with each contraction. Luckily, we had all delivered babies before.

When I arrived at the hospital with Bob, Miriam cried. "You didn't think I would show?" he asked incredulously.

She hiccuped. "I know how insane that sounds, but a part of me did."

He hugged her through her next contraction. "It has always been forever for me, Sassenach."

I slumped in a chair in the waiting room. I felt clammy and needed to rest before getting back into my car. "You look like shit, Jenna," Lucy commented.

I smiled wryly at her. "I feel like shit."

"I hope you're not contagious," Candace sniffed from my other side.

I massaged the back of my neck while bending toward my knees. "Not contagious."

"Oh, I am sure you know that," Candace said sarcastically.

In that moment I was so tired. "Actually, I do."

A hand rubbed my back between the bones of my shoulders. It must have been Lucy's. I didn't think Candace believed me. "How could you possibly?"

"Cancer. It's cancer."

The hand stopped rubbing. "Come again."

I groaned. Why wouldn't my head stop ringing? "I have end-stage renal cancer," I breathed gulping breaths of air, but they didn't seem to enter my bloodstream.

"Why are you just telling us this now?" Candace shrieked.

"Quiet down, everyone is looking," Lucy said. "She must have her reasons."

"I don't give a fuck if everyone is looking. I need explanations."

I would have loved to give her some, but those explanations weren't all that clear at this moment as the oxygen my body desperately wanted wasn't coming. I had kept the secret so long that I couldn't remember why it had started in the first place. Something about not wanting things to change. Something about not wanting to be the object of pity. Something more about the tenuous relationships that needed fixing before I left this world. It all turned to ash as I tried to reason it through now. I just needed to breathe and live to see this new baby born. To see the puppy Candace would replace Paul with. To see my kids get married. I think mostly I just didn't want to talk about it because I didn't want to think about it. I didn't want to live it. I just wanted to live.

Lucy laid me down in her lap on the bench. "It looks like your explanations will have to wait until later. We need to get a nurse over here, and we need to call Clifford."

Lucy stroked her fingers through my hair, which was nice.

***

"What did she tell you?" Voices swim to me in the darkness. I know their owners but I don't have the energy to speak with them yet so I just listen. Cringing at my own stupidity.

Candace: Not a whole hell of a lot.

Clifford: Did she tell you about the book?

Lucy: The what now?

Clifford: Ok, so she didn't tell you.

Candace: Yeah, we get that she has Cancer. Is there something more?

Clifford: She's working on a book for you guys. I tried to get her to tell you about it.

Candace: A Book? That's her big secret, not the fact that she's dying?

Clifford: The book is about you.

Candace: Me?

Clifford: All of you.

Lucy: So I am in it too?

Clifford: And Miriam, and me. She was trying to finish it before the end.

Lucy: The end of what?

Candace: Before she fucking dies on us.

Lucy: Candace, language.

Candace: Oh, you swear worse than I do.

Lucy: I am trying not to.

Candace: So she wrote a book about us, so what?

Lucy: You're not mad?

Candace: I will be made later. Like when she wakes up.

Miriam: Knock. Knock. Is she awake yet?

Lucy: Not yet.

Miriam: I brought someone to meet her.

Candace: She'll just have to wait her turn. Serves her right for keep something this big from us. Give her here.

Lucy: I knew you were mad.

Candace: Not about the book. Oh, look how precious she is. What are you naming her?

Miriam: I haven't decided yet. Is that weird? She's been in this world for two days. We are being discharged today, and this baby still doesn't have a name.

Lucy: My turn. My turn.

I heaved my eyes open. The room was bright. I had to shut my eyes again because the glare was painful after so long with my eyes closed. Had I heard them right? Had it been two days? I blinked, my eyes slowly adjusting. I could hear Clifford's hitched breath, that meant he'd noticed I was awake.

My throat burned like I had swallowed gravel as I tried to speak. "Well, I guess the cat is out of the bag."

My friends looked at me with eyes brimming over. "You are such a bitch, Jenna." Candace greeted me.

"You scared me to death," Miriam chastised.

Lucy snorted while carefully cradling a brown bundle. "You were too busy to be scared."

"Afterward," Miriam sniffed, reaching to take her baby back. Lucy reluctantly let her and I watched as Miriam cradled the sweet bundle as if the baby would bring her comfort instead of the other way around.

Candace had her arms crossed in a tight band across her chest. "So you wrote a book?"

I coughed and Clifford jerked forward ineffectually to comfort me, but not knowing how. He ended up blotting my chin with a cloth even though I didn't need blotting. "It's not finished."

Miriam glanced at the others. "A book? I thought we were mad at her for not telling us about the big C."

Lucy patted her knee. "We are. But Clifford just informed us that she wrote a book about us."

Miriam raised her eyebrows. "What about us?"

Lucy chuckled. "Oh, I have my suspicions."

"Enough about me." I broke into the conversation. "I am here to hold the baby."

Miriam levered herself up from the chair that she'd been slumped in without disturbing the sleeping baby. I watched as Clifford steadied her elbow. She placed the warm wrapped bundle in my arms. This baby smelled so perfect. Like new beginnings. Like every baby I had ever loved and would ever love. Holding this sweet girl right now would probably have to take the place of all of the babies I wouldn't get to hold. Those produced by my daughter and my son. I kissed her on her wrinkled forehead and sighed. It would do.

Lesson Learned: Honesty is the best policy. Those that love you, will love you, anyway.

Chapter 12

Afterward

Though I am not the writer that my wife was, I know anyone reading this would want to know a few things. She and I continued to edit the book from her hospital bed as she grew weaker and weaker from treatments that weren't working. She was determined to leave her friends with something of herself they could look back on fondly rather than the shell she became.

Obviously, the girls were more mad at Jenna for not telling her about the disease than they were about being the subject of a marriage book. They visited often all the way until the end. They have been a life boat to me as I drowned a little each day in my own grief.

Jenna taught me what it was to be a partner, to want to be better than I was for the sake of another. The way she viewed life as an endless experiment will forever shape my interactions with the world I now face without her. For all the lessons she wanted to teach, I know she learned a little she didn't expect to each day from us as much as we learned from her. As you know, her book was published posthumously. It was not how I would have wanted it, but time isn't always on our side.

The ladies continue to meddle in each other's lives and my own just as much as they ever did, which was Jenna's final gift to me: a family chosen by love rather than blood.

Miriam's White Habanero Pepper Chicken Tortilla Soup

2 tablespoons butter or lard

1 teaspoon ground cumin

1 teaspoon chipotle (or chili) powder

1 teaspoon garlic powder

2-3 lbs. boneless skinless chicken thighs

4 garlic cloves

1 onion, diced

1 Anahcim pepper or Hatch Chile, diced

3 White Habanero peppers minced, (6 for a man cold)

4 cups chicken stock

1 teaspoon agave nectar (or honey)

1 teaspoon salt

1 cup water (as necessary)

1 to 1.5 pounds tomatillos, diced

1 Avocado

Tortilla or Tortilla chips

Mexican crema or Sour Cream to taste

Directions:

Start by seasoning the chicken with cumin, chipotle, and garlic powder. Brown the chicken thighs in a large pot with the lard until they are cooked mostly through, about 3 mins a side. Remove and set aside. Then add the peppers, onion, and garlic to the large pot, scraping the browned bits into the vegetables. Cook over high heat for 4 minutes or until the peppers are charred a little.

While the chicken and veggies are cooking on the stove top, lightly oil then broil the diced tomatillos in the oven until they are just splitting, about 6 minutes on high. Allow tomatillos and veggies to come to room temperature, then combine with 1/2 cup of chicken stock to blend into a puree.

Dice or shred the chicken then return the chicken and the puree to the pot. Add the rest of the broth, the nectar and salt. Bring the soup to a simmer. Let simmer for 40 minutes covered, adding water as necessary to achieve desired thickness of the broth.

Top with Salty White Corn Tortilla strips, avocado and Mexican crema.